A KADE CHRISTMAS

A LOGAN AND TAYLOR NOVELLA

TIJAN

Edited by Rogena Mitchell-Jones, RMJ Manuscript Service
Proofread by Paige Maroney Smith, Kara Hildebrand, Kimberley Holm, Chris O'Neil Parece, Serena McDonald
Beta read by Crystal R Solis, Amy English, Eileen Robinson

To all my Fallen Crest and Roussou readers!
Thank you guys. Your support means the world to me.

1

TAYLOR
PRESENT

Positive.

The test was positive. I stared at it for thirty minutes, then turned and vomited my breakfast from that morning.

2

A MONTH EARLIER

"**T**aylor."

I woke to Logan whispering my name, nudging my hip. I peeked through an open eye and stared at him. Nope. It was dark out. It was *still* dark out. I had no clue the time, but I knew it was hellish early in the morning. There's a universal rule. You do not wake a nurse after they've worked a double shift and had stayed *another* three hours for the paperwork.

I loved Logan, but I was ready to kill him, and I knew how. I knew *all the ways* to murder someone.

"I love you, honey, but if you shake me one more time, I am going to take a scalpel to a part of your body and you don't want to know which part." I was lying on my stomach, snuggled into our blankets. I was an RN at the local hospital, and Logan was a partner at his firm. We did well, seriously well, but at that moment, I was grateful for so many of our blessings because this bed was one of the most comfortable places in the world. I glanced out the window, saw that it was starting to snow, and yes, this was my favorite place to be. Here. This bed. With Logan. Knowing I didn't have another shift for a long time! This all happened last minute, today. Another nurse needed to switch schedules, and pick up more hours. I took her hours next month, so score for me.

And again, heaven. Right here.

I closed my eyes and put my head back onto the pillow. "I love you, but leave me alone. I want to sleep."

"Taylor." He wasn't whispering now, and a second later, he whipped my pillow out from under me.

"Logan!"

I reared up—or started to rear up—but Logan caught my hand and flipped my entire body. I had no clue how he did that, but I wasn't surprised. He was seriously efficient at moving my body around. I landed on my back and he was on top of me. His legs straddled mine, and as I growled, raising my other hand, he caught that one too. Then, with both my hands pinned down, his hips sank further onto me, and he leaned down slowly.

God, his eyes. So dark. So filled with the typical Logan mischief.

As long as I'd known him, it was the same look, the one that said, 'I have a great idea that you will probably hate, but you're going to go along with it because I've decided we're going to do it and you love me that much so you'll come along.' It was that look. Everyone fell for it, literally everyone.

I growled, but he half-grinned and half-smirked down at me. "I want to go to Hawaii."

I stilled, frowning. "What?"

"Right now. Today. This hour. I want to go."

Oh, man. Maybe this was one of those moments that I wouldn't mind so much.

We were in our thirties. No children. We were together, but we weren't married.

I never minded. I had Logan. That's all I cared about. He had haunts and his own demons, so I always went with his timeline. Deciding to go to Hawaii on a whim was something we could do.

"What about your work? What about the boys?" I said we

didn't have children, but that didn't mean we didn't have children. Two golden retrievers were in the hallway, and I was shocked that the door was closed. They were whining, wanting to get into bed with us.

Logan's mischievous look just went up a level. "I decided to take some time off and I made a call. Sam said they'd watch them for us."

Samantha was Logan's sister-in-law. They had their own house *full* of kids, the human and four-legged kind. "Are they sure? It's such late notice."

Logan slid his entire body down so he was lying on me, his eyes staring deep into mine. His were starting to smolder, and I felt another piece of him enjoying this position a whole lot. He released one of my hands. That hand went to my hip and slid up under my shirt. "I'm very sure that *they're* very sure."

I laughed, but Logan's mouth was on mine.

Hawaii was going to have to wait a bit.

PRESENT

I was going to be a mom.

Blinking back tears, I was now no longer staring at the pregnancy test. I was holding it, and I was sitting in the bathroom, my back to the shower, and I had tears rolling down my face. I was blinking them back so I could see the pregnancy test, but wow.

Positive.

Mom, I'm going to have a baby.

I hadn't known. After seeing my mom gunned down in front of me and later losing one of my best friends, I had a different outlook on life. Enjoy. Be grateful for your blessings. And love. Always love. So maybe it was because of those events that I was okay with chilling, being happy being with Logan, but I'd been going on his timeline.

He had struggles. I knew he did. I knew. I knew him better than anyone right now.

I knew he feared being like his father.

I knew he feared being absent and cold like his mother.

I knew he worried about marriage, fearing it'd only end in divorce.

Those are all seriously valid struggles, and I waited. I had struggled at times, but I made a conscious decision. I loved my man. I was his ride or die. I'd be at his side, always, but now I was pregnant, and I was in my thirties.

I wasn't waiting anymore.

Oh.

Wow.

Okay.

I touched my stomach, looking down.

Holy fuck, little dude or dudette. You're with me, no matter what. You lucked out. You got this momma as your momma, and I'm going to be the best damn momma I can be. Got that?

I closed my eyes and sent out another thought.

Mom, it'd totally be amazing right now if I could feel you, if I could become psychic and communicate with you. I waited. Nothing. But no, I could smell her perfume, and just like that, *Thanks, Mom. You got a grandchild coming. Tell me you're happy. I love you. I miss you.*

And I swear, I *swear* I could hear her say *I love you* back to me.

Then my phone rang.

Logan calling.

4

EARLIER

The airport was bustling when we got there. The snow wasn't helping, but Logan took my hand and began weaving through the lines. We had premier access to get through the security lines faster, and when we approached, the two workers started smiling.

"Logan, my man." The first guy held his hand up, and Logan met it with his.

"Raj, how's it going?"

The guy's eyebrows shot up. "Same as always. It's going, but how are you? Tell me your brother's team is going to do better this year."

Logan laughed, handing over his ID, and he motioned to me, showing both of our tickets. The other worker, a woman, cleared us both, but she listened to Logan and her coworker have an entire conversation.

The guy's name was Rajdo. After Logan skimmed over talking about Mason's football team, I learned that Rajdo had a wife pregnant with their fifth kid. They were having a hard time planning their older son's Bar Mitzvah, and they needed to head south later in the month for his niece's quinceañera. The woman worker's name was Sandra. She hated Mason's team, but since she knew Mason was Logan's brother, she said he was 'alright' in her books. And she said all that with a wink and a smile my way.

No one else was behind us, but when a couple of guys started down our lane, pulling business carry-ons behind them, we moved into the actual security line.

It was the same effect there, except the workers knew me.

We got so many 'Heya, Logan' and 'Taylor! Why are you still with this guy?' that other passengers began pulling out their phones. One girl's eyes got big, and she started typing fast on her phone.

Logan, by himself, wasn't famous, but because of Mason's football fame, Samantha's Olympic record, and Nate's relation to Blaise DeVroe, some fans online had taken to knowing who everyone was in our group. That included Logan and Nate. Because of all of that, I was guessing the girl was the only one who recognized Logan for being Logan Kade.

"How's the hospital going?" The question came from the last security agent as she waved me through.

I moved aside, grabbed my tote as it came down the conveyor belt, and began putting my items back into my bag. Logan had moved forward to a bench, doing the same.

I shrugged. "It's still there. What can I say?"

She gave me a soft smile, her gaze looking me over. "Well, safe travels wherever you and the mister are going."

I finished up, shrugging on my bag. "Thank you, Tracy."

Her smile got wide.

They wore name tags, but we always tried to go through this security line, and Tracy was studying to be a nurse, so there was an extra connection between us. She always acted like I wouldn't know who she was, but you don't forget a fellow nurse or who's going to be a fellow nurse.

Logan was standing, ready to go, when I got to him. He took my hand, lacing our fingers as we started for our gate.

"How long do we have?"

He glanced at me. "Not long. They start boarding in twenty minutes."

I nodded as we kept going.

Everything was last minute, but Logan and I each traveled so much that we knew the process.

Except for this time, I was finding that I didn't totally.

When we got to the gate, Logan would typically find a place for us to sit, and he'd head off, making the social rounds. He knew the drivers going past or the front desk people. He knew a couple of the maintenance staff.

This time, when we got to the gate, he gave the front desk workers (those who knew him) a hello nod and pulled me over to our own private corner. Or what we could find. There was one seat free, looking out over the tarmac. He put his bag down, took my bag, placed it beside his, then sat down and pulled me to sit on his lap.

His arms draped around me, holding me secure, and he rested his forehead on my shoulder.

I half-turned to him. "You okay?"

He nodded, closing his eyes as I raised my hand, touching the side of his cheek. "Just want you right now."

I loved Logan. I'd always known I loved Logan, and it wasn't a deal where we had a typical 'honeymoon' phase for the first few years. I was in love with him now more than ever. It grew every day, every month, every year. With every touch, every time he reached for my hand, every time he laced our fingers, every time he did things like this, like ignoring the rest of the airport behind us, pulling me to his lap, and then saying things like that. But not just saying it, meaning it.

He meant it.

A rush of warmth melted my insides, and I leaned down, giving him a small kiss. "I love you."

He turned, his eyes smiling and so eternally warm. He found my mouth again.

We kissed a few more times, ignoring some of the comments from others, and after a bit, he just held me in his lap as we waited.

I was starting to have a feeling this trip was different from the others.

5

PRESENT

I was nervous. Maybe I shouldn't have been, but I was.

Logan had expressed his concern over having kids many times. There'd been talks, late-night discussions into the early hours of the morning, so I understood his fear.

I didn't have the same fear. When I loved, I loved with everything in me. I knew I would try to be the best mother I could be, but Logan had different feelings.

I had to respect his fears, but this was a done deal.

I'd gone to the doctor. It was confirmed.

I even had a tentative inception date.

The doctor was the first to give me congratulations.

I waited to tell anyone. Not my father. Not Samantha. Not anyone.

It was Logan first. He was my best friend, and it was the night to do it, and I was shaking.

I made dinner, tacos for us, and yeah, my arms were *actually* shaking.

Then my phone pinged an alert.

Logan: Running late! Something's going on with Dad so I have to head to Mason's.

Logan: You should eat without me. I'll grab something there.

Logan: Are you okay? You haven't texted me much today.

I drew in a breath, one to calm my nerves.

Crap. What do I do here?

Tell him to come home instead? That would alarm him. He'd do it, but he'd come in wondering if something was wrong. I didn't want to tell him like that.

But... if something was going on with his family, it could take days or weeks before a good time came up for me to tell him.

I needed to wait. I would wait.

The next time he was home, I'd tell him.

Me: I'm good. I'll cuddle up with the boys tonight and watch TV. Let me know what's going on when you know.

Logan: You want me to swing by and pick you up? We can bring the boys with us to Mason's? Do dinner there instead. Sam won't care. Maddie will love it.

Normally, yes. I'd be all over that.

Logan's brother and sister-in-law were amazing. His nieces and nephew too. Barring his parents, Logan had a great family around him.

But not tonight. I wanted my own boys around me, and I'd wait to tell him.

Me: I'm tired or I would. Kinda want to chill with the pups tonight.

Logan: Okay. I'll hurry home as soon as I can. Love you.

Me: Love you too.

Me: I made tacos, by the way.

Logan: OMG! Now you tell me!

6

EARLIER

He did sweet things the entire flight to L.A. and then to Hawaii.

He held my hand the whole time.

He walked with me when I got up to go to the bathroom.

He went and got me water or coffee when he knew I was about to go and get some myself. Just very simple but thoughtful things. It was a continuous cycle. Not that Logan wasn't like this usually. He was always sweet to me, always doing considerate things, but when we were around others, it was about the others. He thrived off that interaction. I usually got this treatment behind closed doors. Which was how we both preferred it, but I wasn't complaining about this treatment—hell to the no.

He carried my bags for me, and he knew I didn't care. A backpack was a backpack. We tended to both pack light on purpose. It was easier to grab and go than wait for baggage claim.

He had a rental ready for us at the airport, a luxury Escalade.

When we got to the house that we shared with Mason, Nate, and Matteo, I was blown away again.

Pink rose petals lined the sidewalk into the house, into the front entryway and led out to the back sitting area by the pool.

We were right on the beach in Oahu, but we still had an infinity pool, and the rose petals filled the entire back section.

Logan came up behind me, his hand touching my hip as he molded himself to my back. He folded his arms around me. I could only shake my head, my throat clogging up with emotion. So much emotion.

I saw champagne. I saw tacos. I saw flowers everywhere.

"Is it our anniversary, and I forgot?"

He laughed, his breath caressing my ear. "No. I just wanted to do something for you."

I looked up, meeting his gaze. "Are you dying? Is *someone* dying?"

He grinned again, shaking his head. "No." His eyes turned dark, smoldering, and his mouth moved down. His lips found mine, a gentle and tender kiss. "I don't have to be anything with you."

I turned so my front was pressed to his. His hands slid down, grasping my ass. He held me there, holding me in place, still looking down at me. "I don't have to be funny. I don't have to be sarcastic. I don't have to fight. You let me be just me, and I don't think I fully express how much I am thankful for that."

I reached up, cupping his face.

A tear slipped free from his right eye, and I brushed it away with my thumb. "I'm not sure what brought this on, but I am seriously loving it." I pulled him down, his forehead to mine, and I closed my eyes. "I am fully aware of all the roles you play with your friends and family at your job." I linked our left hands together, bringing them to my mouth. "You are their protector, but I'm your protector. You're their shield, but I'm your shield. I will always unconditionally love you. I always have."

I opened my eyes, looked up, and saw more unshed wetness brimming in his eyes.

I had no clue what was going on, what brought on this trip,

but I flattened my other hand against Logan's chest and felt his heart pounding hard. Whatever it was, it was important to him.

I lifted on my toes, my arms going around his neck, and as one unit because we'd done this so much, he reached to catch me as I lifted. My legs wound around his waist. He held me there, dropping his head to brush against my cheek, and he whispered, "Taylor?"

"Hmmm?" I loved how his fingers were moving over my ass, caressing me. I tightened my legs.

He groaned but added, still a hoarse whisper, "Will you marry me?"

———

I ANSWERED him as I kissed him that night.

As he carried me to the bedroom.

As he placed me down on the bed, taking my clothes off.

As I did the same, kissing him as I removed each piece of clothing.

I answered him in the way that we made love that night.

Tender and sensual caresses.

It was slow when he slid in me, looking into my eyes, never looking away as he began moving inside of me. I gasped, my head fell back when he touched my mouth, running his hand down my throat, and circling the back of my head, still moving in me.

I never stopped watching him.

He continued thrusting, his hands holding my face, his forehead touching mine, and my legs wrapped tightly around his waist, my hips rolling with him.

He kept going, deeper and deeper.

A sheen of sweat broke out over both of our bodies.

We breathed each other in.

He never stopped looking into me until we both finally

crested, our bodies shaking together, coming apart, and then we rested.

He didn't slide out of me.

He waited, still inside of me, still holding my face, his forehead on mine. He ran his thumb over the side of my face, both sides, both dipping into my mouth as he lifted his head, moving until his mouth covered mine.

I closed my eyes for the first time as he kissed me.

This was a literal showing of love between us.

I never unwound my legs from him.

I moved, my hands wrapping around his as he held me, and after a bit, the kiss grew more demanding, more urgent, more commanding. I felt him hardening inside of me, and even then, he waited. We kept kissing. He ran his hand down my side, over my arm, across my stomach, and circling one of my breasts. He moved his thumb over my nipple and then pulled away, his mouth leaving mine. He arched over me, his mouth finding my nipple instead. He moved his hand down, pressing over my clit. Rubbing. Teasing.

He kept sucking on my breast, his tongue caressing me.

I moaned, my head falling back to the pillow as I felt all the pleasure he was giving me.

Then he pulled out, flipped me over, and all those sensual and slow touches were gone. I felt him fully hard and demanding behind me. He positioned me on my knees, angled down, and ran a hand up my back, going to my ass. He moved in behind me, lining up.

"I'm going to fuck you hard."

Another moan left me. "Yesss."

As his thumb went in my ass, he sheathed his cock inside of me.

I was a writhing mess.

Yes. Yes. Just *yes*.

STILL EARLIER

We had an entire vacation in Hawaii.

Logan showed me the ring the following day. It was a petite twist, 14k rose gold round diamond. I swooned, and I wasn't a swooner, but this ring—I was swooning so much.

And blinking back tears because I never thought this would happen.

Logan slipped it onto my finger as he got back in bed, and I asked him, my voice raspy, "Are you sure?"

He paused, staring at me, and a whole different look came over him. A look of wonder, tenderness, and gentleness came over him. If he'd had any stress that morning, all of it had melted as he pulled me back into his arms. He pressed his lips to my forehead, pulling me to his chest. "Yes. God, yes. I'm sure. I don't deserve you. Of *that*, I'm sure."

Well, okay then.

———

WE DIDN'T LEAVE the bed, not until our stomachs were growling. We ordered salads, giving the tacos a brief break.

PRESENT

S
o there was a whole shindig with James Kade.

Logan and Mason both needed to fly to Fallen Crest.

Logan told me what was going on, but I was in this whole zen mood here. I listened, and I was there for him for whatever he needed. Encouragement. Cheering. If he needed me to kick him in the ass, whatever he needed, I gave it, but also, I'm still trying to stay in the Zen mode.

No drama.

James Kade was *only* drama, but Logan and Mason had it under control. They always did what was necessary whenever they needed to get something under control.

Samantha brought the kids over. We didn't live far, so it wasn't hard to get everyone in the car. Maddie helped a ton, and we had an entire toy room for the twins when they got here. I liked having them here because it was my way of trying to do something nice for Samantha.

I made dinner. Samantha had some wine. I had non-alcoholic wine. She didn't notice.

We laughed. She asked me about work. I asked how her

training was going because she'd decided to try for one last run for the Olympics.

During the visit, Heather called, and I left her alone to talk with her best friend.

I went and played hide-and-go-seek with the twins while getting the 411 from Maddie. There was a boy—*ick, hiss*—who liked her. I asked if she liked him back, and she thought about it, then shrugged and said, "I don't know, but if he doesn't stop messaging me about how nice my hair is, I'm going to punch him." She paused and added, "I'll do it after school so I don't embarrass him in front of his friends." She finished, giving me a long and dramatic nod while sharing a look as if to say, *'You feel me, sister?'*

I learned when Maddie was born to always agree with her. She was a female incarnate of Logan and Mason together.

"I feel you, sister."

She harrumphed and sighed before standing up. "Okay. It's my turn to find the little shits. You stay, take a load off, Aunt Taylor."

I still hadn't told Logan.

EARLIER

We kayaked.
                We surfed.
We hiked.
We went horseback riding.
We snorkeled.
We enjoyed poke.
We had a luau on our second to last night.
We did everything tourists were supposed to do. We did it. It wasn't our first time in Hawaii, and it wouldn't be our last, but there was an extra frenzy about the trip. We needed to do all of this for ourselves, like this was our trip, for us, and we were exploring Hawaii for the first time.

It was our last night, and we were in bed. Neither of us wanted to leave. Or move.

Logan lay between my legs, his arms spread out. I was almost cradling him, running my hands through his hair. He nestled his head just under my breasts, and every once in a while, he liked to reach up and touch my breast or my nipple or kiss there.

"I don't want to go back."

He took in a deep breath, then let it out. His body sank even more into the bed and me. "Me neither."

His phone lit up from the bedside stand.

It'd been lighting up for the last few days, and Logan was *not* being Logan. He was ignoring every text, email, message, and call. He wasn't responding to anyone.

I'd been feeling the urgency from him since he proposed. It was deep inside of him, but I could feel it. It was almost desperation, but I didn't know what it was for or from. I hadn't the heart to bring it up, not wanting to interrupt our trip and this sanctuary atmosphere we were in.

I closed my eyes, my hands pausing then going through his hair, and I knew I had to bring it up now. "Do you need to get that?"

He was shaking his head even before I finished the question, rolling and burrowing into me even more, his head fully facing down. He raised himself up while his head stayed. His back arched. His hands found my hips as his hips moved up to mine. "No."

The phone lit up again.

I frowned. "What's going on?"

"I don't know, and I don't want to know." He lifted his head again, his eyes tormented. "Not today. Not this trip. I'll deal with it when we go back, but not before."

I closed my mouth, a wave of pain rose from feeling his pain.

He whispered, his forehead resting to mine again, "I want to get married now. You and me. No one else. I want this for us, *only* us."

A tear slipped out because this Logan rarely came out. It was when he knew something was happening, something from his family or his friends or his job, that would pull him away. He always went. He put them ahead of himself and me, but it was how Logan was.

I knew this going in. I didn't care. It was a part of him that I fell in love with.

I didn't want him any other way. I only wanted him to be Logan, so he needed to do what he needed to do to be himself—if that made any sense.

Feeling his pain now, I slid my fingers through his hair, palming his head as he lifted up and stared at me. His eyes were haunted on a trip when they shouldn't be.

"Okay."

The troubled look vanished. "Yeah?" He started to smile.

I nodded, whispering back, "Yes. You and me."

His eyes closed, but his phone lit up. This time it started buzzing on the bedside stand. Someone was calling. It wasn't just a message or an alert.

Logan cursed, rolled over, looked at his phone, and turned it off. "Not today. Not this day."

He put the phone back, looked at me, searing me with his need.

I was ready for him as he reached for me.

So the shindig with James ended up being more than a shindig. It was a whole cluster fuck. The big D (divorce) word was being thrown around, which escalated to Analise flying to Boston and staying at Samantha's. Which... wasn't going well.

Mason and Logan were flying back and forth from Fallen Crest to here every few days. Mason had practices and games, so he went when he could. He ended up calling Nate to help tag-team with Logan.

My man called every night, and he sounded more and more exhausted with each phone call. Because of that, I asked around, got my schedule flipped, and got plenty of time off. Score for nurses helping each other out. I called Samantha, letting her know the situation, that I was going to head to Fallen Crest as a surprise. Sam was down to help make that happen. She offered to watch the boys, but I called in other favors with them too. Like Logan, our two pups were heavily loved. We had a whole adopted grandmother two houses down that the dogs visited, and most of the time, it was without our knowledge. We found out about the relationship when she texted me once, asking how the boys were because they hadn't seen her in a few days. (That was a time when Sam and Mason were watching them for us.) And I had a whole surreal moment because I thought she was talking about human boys, not our boys.

Nonetheless, we figured it out, and now the pups loved spending time with their very own grandmama. I'd include her husband, but he liked to complain about why he was still buying dog treats three years after their last dog died—just kidding. The grandpa was very much included. Matty liked to climb up into his lap. It was only a problem when he wasn't sitting.

I liked to joke that they got that side from their dad, not myself.

I digress—back to my amazing surprise. I was now on the plane (after another hello to Tracy and all the security guards asking about Logan, asking what Mason's actual chances were at winning their first playoff game), and I was settled in.

I needed to tell Logan about the baby.

I was still waiting, but it never seemed the right time.

He'd not been home to spend a full evening with me in so long, and I kept holding off, thinking the time would come.

Now it would.

I was going to him. We'd have so much time.

I needed to plan how to tell him.

I LANDED, and the surprise was on me.

Logan was there but not to pick me up.

He was there to pick up Quincey, who was flying in to surprise Nate.

EARLIER

LOGAN

G od, Taylor was fucking beautiful.

Every morning, every day, every evening, she took my breath away. She was raw. She was genuine. She was never demanding. She was strong. She was supportive. She knew when to fight, when to love, when to avoid, and when to stand.

She'd been through things that I never wanted to imagine. Ever. But she was here, and she was walking toward me. Barefoot. Nighttime. On a beach in Hawaii. She had flowers in her hair—flowers in her hands. A line of lights marked the path to me, where I was standing. The waves were coming in behind us, and I couldn't take my eyes off of her.

I loved her. I loved her so fucking much.

I wasn't Mason.

I never had to be the one to make the hard decisions, not early on, not like him. I didn't like feeling emotions. I used sex to push everything away, and because of that, it crippled me at times. I hadn't processed our parents' horrendous divorce, how they treated each other growing up. That's what I learned. That's what I saw love was.

Mason got his woman right away. He hid in her.

I hid in sex, drinking, and fighting. And none of it was ever enough for me.

I met Taylor in college, and I still didn't want to deal with shit.

She loved me despite it all, and I knew she should've walked away from me so long ago. She never did.

Mason was strong. Samantha was strong. I'm strong, but fuck everyone because Taylor was the strongest. She endured, and she keeps smiling, and she keeps loving. There'd been a few times when she got worried about things, spoke up, stopped me from doing something stupid, but for the most part, she just loved.

She was coming toward me now, her eyes bright and shining, and she was wearing some sort of dress. She informed me she wanted off-white, but fuck if I knew the reason. She had one, and she tried to explain it in a very articulate way, but I was only fantasizing about taking it off of her. There was a slit up her leg, and as soon as I could, my hand was going there and going up to find its landing strip.

"Are you ready for this?"

I couldn't tear my eyes away, but I responded to the minister. "Never been more ready."

Then she was in front of me, and she was blinking back tears. I moved in, catching some of those tears and brushing them away. I smiled. "Hi."

She laughed, a few more tears falling free. "Hiya back."

The minister cleared his throat. "Are you both ready?"

Taylor answered this time, "Oh, boy am I."

Her cheeks flushed, but I stepped into her and touched my lips to hers.

I never wanted them to leave.

She startled, not expecting my kiss, but softened and leaned into me. Her hand slid up my chest, rounding my neck, and I continued to kiss her because I could. This was my woman.

After a few more seconds, after I knew I had kissed away her embarrassment, I stepped back and motioned to the minister. "We're ready."

He started.

PRESENT
LOGAN

"I s everything okay with Taylor?"

Nate asked that question as we were in the backyard of James' house. He'd technically moved to a different house, saying this gigantic mausoleum was Mason's and mine, but we both refused to claim it. For a bit, we tried to VRBO it, but that fell through. Too many parties. Too much damage. The neighborhood hadn't liked that either, so here we were, back here. But hearing Nate's question, I turned and studied Taylor a bit.

She and Quincey were laughing, sitting across from us. They'd gone in to mix drinks for everyone. Taylor insisted on handing them out, but they hadn't returned to sit with us for some reason.

I studied her a bit, noticing she was holding her back. It was in her posture. She was sitting rigid, a little more guarded than necessary, and I almost wanted to punch Nate because fuck him for noticing when I hadn't, but that was on me.

I cursed, sitting forward slowly.

Nate snorted and started laughing.

I growled. "Shut up, you asshat."

"Way to take care of your woman."

I flipped him off, not caring one bit how old we were. I'd flip off anyone who wanted to scold me on that crap too.

"You guys going to go see her dad?"

I nodded, not having asked Taylor but already knowing. "We always do."

"If she wants to go alone?"

He was digging at me, and I glared at him. "You know I won't let her do that."

He was biting back a grin but sobered and nodded in the direction of the house. "Where's your dad tonight?"

I snorted. "Ironically, David's on James Kade babysitting duty."

Nate's eyes got big. "Analise's ex-husband is helping to watch over the current husband? I knew it was bad when you first called me in, but man. I had no idea it was that bad that even Malinda and David got pulled into this shit."

I sighed, remembering the first phone call, and my gut tightened. "If he had only cheated on her, it might not have been this bad, but it wasn't just a cheat. It was a full second family. Mason and I have two little brothers with another mother who wants nothing to do with James, Mason, or me. And Helen is her fucking best friend, spewing only God knows what hatred for our dad."

"He didn't just lose 100k. He lost the whole fucking bank, in other words."

I nodded, feeling my gut shriveling up and tightening and starting to try to swallow itself.

I wasn't James Kade.

I wouldn't be James Kade.

I'd never do that shit to Taylor.

Ever.

I just needed to believe it now.

But first things first, I stood and glanced at Nate. "I need to figure out what's going on with my woman."

He gave me a slight nod back. "Why the fuck are you still standing here? Do an eighth of what that woman does for you and take care of her. Clean her jar."

I threw him a frown because what the fuck?

He just smiled at me, tipping his beer back and taking a drag.

Okay then.

Mission Clean Her Jar was about to commence, whatever that meant.

13

TAYLOR

Logan was coming my way, and I knew that face. He realized something was 'off' with me, and he was coming to fix it, no matter what it was.

No, no, no.

I needed to tell him about the baby, but not tonight, not here, not in this way.

I knew. I just knew he was feeling certain ways because of the recent James Kade drama, and I could see the second-guessing eating at him.

He was scared he would hurt me how his dad had hurt the women in his life, but Logan never got it. Not completely.

Logan would never do what his dad had done. And because he was so scared of that, he went overboard sometimes helping others because he didn't want to be his dad in any way.

I didn't want to tackle that issue tonight.

I didn't want to be the one to turn the tables and scrape away his struggles, but I also didn't want to tell him about the baby.

I wanted that night to be amazing and perfect, and tonight in Fallen Crest, when we weren't alone, it wasn't that night.

I don't know. Maybe I was being stupid. Perhaps I should just blurt it out, but Logan didn't want children. He had told me going into so much detail about how he never wanted to do to his children what his parents had done to him and Mason.

I got it.

So yeah. I was still hoping for the perfect night, though. But I was starting to think that night would never happen.

He came over and pulled me to my feet. He took my drink, handing it to Quincey as he said something to her. I assumed it was something along the lines that we were going to bed for the night. I didn't know. I wasn't listening. My heart was pumping so loud in my ears that I couldn't hear anything he was saying.

My blood was coursing through my body.

My vision was blurring.

I was so nervous, so scared.

What would he do when I told him?

How would he react?

We were married.

Would he want to get *unmarried*?

I couldn't tell him. Not yet.

Just not yet.

One more night.

It'd be a better tomorrow.

Yeah. Tomorrow.

He took my hand, lacing our fingers together, and I smiled at the gesture because I always loved that so much.

He led me back into the house, to our room, and before he could start his questions, I moved into him. I silenced him and tonight was my night. I wanted to feel him all night long.

I'd tell him tomorrow.

14

EARLIER

Mrs. Logan Kade.

I couldn't get over that. My new name would be Taylor Kade.

"Morning, *Wife*." Logan came in, carrying coffee for both of us, and handed one over as he got back into bed.

I took it, sipped, and knew there was a whole cheesy glow all over me. "Morning, *Husband*."

His eyes darkened. He tugged me over to him, taking my coffee and setting both of ours on his bedside stand. Then he turned to me and brushed some of my hair from my forehead. "I don't want to go back."

We were supposed to fly back today. We would need to head to the airport in a few hours.

"I know. Me neither."

"I miss the boys, though."

I shared his grin. "Me too."

His eyes grew distant, and he moved into me, burrowing his head into my neck and shoulder. His hand went to my hip, pulling me even more into him before lying flat on my stomach like he was holding me in place. "Can we not tell the others?"

I moved my head so I could see him better. "Keep it a secret?"

He was watching me, concerned, and he nodded slowly. "There's something about keeping it secret. It's just for you and me. No one else has an opinion or advice, or constructive warnings. I mean, you know my deal. My dad was a literal piece of shit to my mom, and he's not the greatest to Analise right now, though he says he's changed. James. Helen. Thank God for Malinda and David. Those are my parent figures. I know it's time to get over the childhood damage, but I don't think some of that shit ever leaves you."

His eyes were troubled.

I reached over, smoothing a hand over his cheek, trying to literally wipe away the concern that he had. I leaned over, whispering as I touched my lips to his, "I'm down for whatever you want. We never have to tell a soul, except my dad, or we can rent a plane to fly a banner over all of Boston."

His eyes grew warm. "Thank you."

It was decided.

We flew back to Boston, and it felt like we were traveling in our own cocoon.

15

PRESENT
TAYLOR

I needed to go in for a prenatal visit, and I *still hadn't told Logan*. This was getting *ridiculous*, but we were in Fallen Crest.

James showed up at the house trashed, so Logan and Nate were dispatched. Something else new happened or came to light. At this point, I was assuming it was some new drama that James couldn't keep quiet. Either way, Logan's father was a mess. The man was broken, which was ironic because he'd created the shitstorm, and he was the biggest baby about it all.

Since James was at the house, Quincey and I were sent to Malinda's house. David had gone over to help the guys out. There was talk about packing, putting a house on the market, and again, the D-word was issued.

"This is insane," Malinda announced as she, Quincey, and I were sitting at the table. She looked between us. "This fucker has ruined lives, but there are two new little ones in the family, and he's crying that his life is over. He is a literal fucker. I want to drink, and I'm not really affected by all this." She reached for her phone. "Who's with me? I'm calling Heather. I want to see where she is, and then we're calling Samantha and Analise. It's time the women all get together, and we figure out how to deal with this asshole." She brought up Heather's number, dialed her, and glanced at both of us. "You in?"

I was affirmative whenever it came to Malinda, to anything Malinda wanted to do.

Quincey followed my lead. "I'm in."

"Good," Malinda grunted.

Heather answered then, "Mama Malinda!"

"I'm calling a Women's Meeting. Are you in town? I'm here with Taylor and Quincey."

Heather's voice dropped, getting serious. "I'm at Manny's, actually. You guys wanna come over? I can close up the back just for us. Ava's here too, and it sounds like she needs some fellow female time."

"We're on the way. Give your bestie a call."

"Will do."

Malinda signed off and stood, grabbing her purse. It was then I realized she meant business.

Oh, boy.

I hadn't thought this through.

Manny's meant booze, and it wasn't the deal where I could be in charge of the alcohol and sneak my own non-alcoholic stuff. Of course, I could tell Heather, but it still felt wrong.

I needed to tell Logan asap. This was getting out of hand.

"You two coming?" Malinda was already at the door.

I realized Quincey was still at the table, watching me with a slight frown. Her eyebrows were pinched together. She leaned over, asking in a low voice, "You okay?"

I jerked my head up. "Yes." My voice came out louder than I intended. I stood up, the chair scraping behind me. "Yes, I'm ready. Sorry. I just realized"—the perfect lie came to me—"I can't drink. I messed up on some medication I was taking for an infection I had."

"What's this?" Malinda migrated back to us.

I repeated the lie, feeling like an arsehole. "I'm so sorry. I can't drink, but wait. I'll be the driver."

Quincey's eyebrows remained pinched together, and she bit down on her bottom lip.

Malinda shrugged, turning around. "Works for me. I'm ready to tear into that weasel, so let's get me drunk and happy before I do."

Quincey waited for me to follow after Malinda, and I tried to give her a reassuring smile, but I didn't think she was buying it. Her frown only deepened.

Oh, man.

If Quincey was getting suspicious, she could voice whatever she was thinking to Nate, he'd say it to Logan, and I knew Logan wouldn't be deterred another night.

Suddenly I was pro-let's-tear-into-the-weasel with Malinda.

HEATHER WAS ready for us when we showed up. She greeted us at the door with two margaritas in hand. Malinda took one, breezing past her. Quincey glanced my way but took the other.

Heather told me, "I got more coming. No worries."

"Nope." Malinda raised her glass in the air. "Taylor got a mix-up with some medication. She's the driver tonight, but that means more for us! So, where's little Ava? Let's handle her shit before we start plotting against Weasel James Kade."

Heather frowned at me but was distracted by Malinda. "What?"

Malinda was leading the way to the back section at Heather's bar. She said over her shoulder, "You said little Ava needs some girl time. That usually means there's a guy involved, and he fucked up royally. Let's handle her stuff before I launch into how we all need to handle the other weasel."

"Uh—"

Malinda had kept going, and we heard a moment later, "There you are, dearie. Tell us who we gotta add to our weasel shitting-on list today, and consider it done."

Quincey stopped and turned back to where Heather and I still were just inside the door. The rest of Manny's was busy, like always, and I noticed her brother was watching us from behind the bar.

Quincey asked, "She's always like this?"

Heather and I nodded as if we were one person.

I heard her brother start laughing. "I'm closing up, Heather. You got your hands full with Mama Malinda tonight."

She glanced at him, but I moved forward.

Malinda wasn't alone. I wanted to hear what was going on with Ava too. She'd been one of Heather's workers, and from all our trips to Fallen Crest, I'd gotten a soft spot for her. She was always in the background, always working since she had so many jobs in town and the neighboring town, and she was attending the local community college. Whoever had hurt Ava was going down.

I was a bit fierce in my love for the girl, a young woman by now.

I also might've been projecting some mama-love here too, but I wasn't going to focus on that until I'd told Logan about the baby.

Until then, Ava.

16

EARLIER

I t had been snowing when we left, and it was snowing when we arrived.

Logan held my hand the whole drive home, stopping to get the boys on the way. As soon as we got home, stepping inside our warm house, Logan stopped me and pulled me into his arms.

He pressed a kiss to my forehead. "I love you."

I tipped my head back, that same warm cheesy glow spreading throughout me again. "I love you too."

We were home. We were married.

We were happy.

17

PRESENT

Ava was done with men, it seemed.

She announced this between margarita number three and margarita number four. By the time she was onto number five, she was on the phone texting with someone. Malinda wanted to know who the guy was so she could break an umbrella over his head. Ava wouldn't tell, saying, "It's someone you know, and I don't want to ruin things for him. He and I were never supposed to even happen. It's all so dumb."

By margarita six, she was gone.

I saw her slip out the back door as a truck pulled up.

My guess, she got horny, and the guy was back in the picture.

With Ava gone, Malinda was onto the next project: Weasel James Kade.

Now, what she did, I wouldn't have done, but it was Malinda, and everyone did what Malinda told them to do.

She called Helen, who was friends with James' whoever-she-was-to-him-now, and Malinda found out they were in Fallen Crest. So, everyone could guess by now what happened. Malinda invited them to Manny's, stating over the phone, "It's better if she meets the girls first because the woman's involved, and you know it. Get her here while we're all still able to stand."

Helen, who didn't do anything anyone told her, did what Malinda told her.

She brought the new woman who had two sons who were Logan's half-brothers, and when she came through the door, my gut fell out through the bottom of my stomach.

It was Tate Sullivan, who was also Logan's ex.

All eyes went to me.

I was on the phone outside of Manny's, trying not to lose my shit. "You were never told *who* your father impregnated?"

Logan was on the other end. "No. He wouldn't tell us. Analise wouldn't say either. Or Helen. Why?"

Good because I wanted to be the one to tell him, "It's your fucking ex-girlfriend."

My Zen was gone.

I had a prenatal appointment scheduled the next day. I still hadn't told Logan about the baby. We'd been married a month now, and my calm Zen was totally and completely destroyed.

I wanted to kill this bitch, and this was me.

I was nice. I was kind. I was strong.

I was the fucking foundation for Logan so he could handle all his shit in life.

Not. Any. More.

I was officially about to blow a gasket, and no one had ever seen me blow a gasket except Logan.

"Logan Kade, get your ass here and handle this bitch or get ready to post my bail because I am. Not. Fucking. Calm right now."

I could hear him draw in a deep breath. "Where are you right now?"

"I am outside of Manny's, and I can see a shovel at Heather's old house, on the porch. I'm thinking of ten different ways I can use that shovel to disembowel your ex-girlfriend. How *the fuck* did this happen?"

He expelled another less restrained breath. "My father, that's how this happened. Don't do anything. We're coming right now."

I hung up because I was done listening to him.

He would come here. He would do what Logan usually did. He'd threaten, throw around a lot of legal jargon, but he'd go head to head against that woman inside, and I *saw* her.

She had fully and completely planned all of this, and she was smirking deep inside. I could see the smugness in her gaze when she saw me, right before she masked it and her bottom lip started trembling.

Helen only saw that last part and swept her to her side, becoming what? The protective mother *now*? To *her*?

I'd met Tate before, on a few trips when we visited Fallen Crest.

She was a snake. Not even. She was a viper.

I was going to lose my shit.

Nope.

Done.

I'd already lost it.

I stepped away from the wall, turned, and went inside.

Commence losing my shit: *now*.

We could hear the yelling from outside.

Nate glanced my way, but I was already running. That was Taylor, and I'd never heard Taylor like that. Her voice was almost shrill.

We shoved inside, heading to the back, and we both had to stop to take a second to process what we were seeing.

Taylor was being held back by Brandon, who was glaring at Heather, who was laughing, bent over beside them. Malinda was adjacent to Taylor, not being held back, but one of Channing's guys was standing in front of her. She had her finger pointing over, no. Wait. She couldn't reach over him. I think it was Moose standing there (he was named for a reason), so she leaned around him, pointing at... Tate.

Fucking Tate.

She was standing on the other side, my mother next to her. Helen (who was my mother in case that needed to be explained, and that said something right there) looked perpetually confused. She was looking between Malinda and Tate and back again. I noticed she was not looking at Taylor.

Fucking Helen. Seriously.

And Tate was now looking at me, and fuck her because I saw the smug look in her gaze.

She was the one my dad impregnated? I was thinking hell no to that whole story, but just as I was heading for Taylor, the screen door opened and Mark Decraw walked in.

"Mom!" he yelled, but he wasn't alone.

His woman came in behind him, or I thought she was still his woman? Cassandra was glaring right alongside him, but at Tate, who hadn't stopped looking at me since noticing I was here.

Malinda was saying, ignoring her son, "*I* am their mother! How can *you* stand by *her* side? How can you not know the history?"

Helen's frown deepened, but then all eyes snapped to me, and I ignored everyone, going right to Taylor.

Brandon saw me and moved aside.

I moved in, taking Taylor into my arms—or I would've.

She shoved off of me, looking over me. "You are a piece of work. *Piece* of *work*. This whole thing was fabricated. I don't believe for a second that you had James Kade's children. It's a scam. I can't believe you. *Fucking* desperate. You still want Logan? Is that it?"

"Logan, get your woman under control—"

I whirled around, finding my mother who had said that. "Shut up. You don't ever talk about my wife like that—"

There was a group gasp, or what sounded like one.

"Wife!"

No clue who that was.

"What?"

Or that.

Heather whispered, almost in awe, "This is so epic."

"Logan." Taylor's hand dropped to my arm, her eyes big.

I winced but pulled her close. "Sorry. I let it slip."

"No." She shook her head, her hand sliding around to the

back of my neck. She moved in closer, and our foreheads rested against each other.

I needed this. I needed her.

Just a touch. A moment. I needed to connect to her.

Taylor was my anchor, and as I got older, it only grew with every day.

I dropped my voice low. "Are you okay that slipped out?"

The anger was gone, and she moved her head up and down gently. She was watching me back, intently. "I'm always okay doing what you want to do, but the secret's out."

I closed my eyes, feeling a ball of tension start to unfold inside my chest.

It'd been there for a while, ever since we found out what my dad had done, but we hadn't known who then. It didn't matter. It took me away from her, and it felt like forever since I had been on the same page with her. I knew something was up, but she didn't want to talk about it last night.

I hadn't pushed.

Now, though. Now our time was done. Everyone would want to know everything, and I didn't want to do that. It was our secret, ours—no one else's. It ceased just being yours when you shared that information, and I wanted to whisk Taylor off.

I wanted to get in the vehicle and drive all the way back to Boston.

I could technically do it.

Nate was here. We could call in favors or just let James deal with his fuck-up.

God.

I was so tempted to do it, let someone else deal with the shit for once.

I pulled Taylor into my chest. My head was buried in the crook of her neck and shoulder, and my arms were wrapped tightly around her. I felt her start to tremble, and her hands slid up the front of my chest, taking hold, forming fists in my shirt.

"Logan." She turned her head, her whisper coming out in a rasp next to my ear.

She almost sounded agonized. Her body kept trembling, and without thinking, I smoothed a hand up her back, going to cup the back of her neck.

Whatever it was would be all right.

Anything.

I loved her. It didn't matter—"I'm pregnant."

19

EARLIER

M y phone was ringing. The clock showed that it was five-thirty in the morning.

I was going to kill my brother.

Grabbing it on the second ring, right as Taylor started to move around, I meant to decline.

A second later, Mason's voice came from my nightstand, "Logan?"

I growled but hurried out of bed, taking the phone with me. "Shh."

The boys had wanted to stay in the room with us last night, and both were on the bed.

I paused, staring at them for a second. Usually, Natty liked to be on the bed while Matty was content to be on the floor. He didn't like our feet moving around. Both usually left with whoever was up first. Taylor had an evening shift, so I was the first up, but my god, I was hoping to get back to bed. I had another hour I could rest.

This morning, though, neither of the boys moved. Both remained right where they were. I had moved so Natty moved to stretch out where I'd been, but they watched me as I left.

Okay then.

I pulled the door closed and went to the guest bathroom, then hit speakerphone as I closed the door. "Why the fuck are you calling at five in the morning?"

I stood over the toilet as Mason answered, "Uh—" He laughed. "Gonna admit that I forgot that normal people don't get up at this time of the day. Sorry. Wait—"

I started pissing.

"Are you pissing right now?"

"You woke me up. Deal with it." I let it flow. *Be free, pee. Be free.* "What do you want?"

"Christmas is coming up—"

I finished pissing.

Mason paused, then continued as I flushed, "James sent me an email last night inviting us out there."

"Nope." I went to wash my hands.

"I know, but shut up. Let me finish. I'm not calling because of that. I'm calling because he never asks us out there. I think something's up."

I paused, right before turning the sink back off, and then grabbed the towel. "Last time he had issues, it was with his business."

"He never asked us for a holiday for that."

I was starting to get a bad feeling in my gut. "I don't like this."

"Me neither, but a heads-up, I guess. Anyways, since you actually answered, Sam wants to do Christmas the day after my game."

"You play on Christmas, right?"

"Yeah, and Sam's heading to the game. She's thinking of inviting Nate and Quincey."

I was nodding and remembered he couldn't see me. "Cool, cool. That sounds good to me."

"Can you guys bring the meat?"

"Sure." I grabbed up the phone again. "Is this really the

reason you called? A heads-up at five in the morning because something might be up with James? And to ask about Christmas Day meat?"

He laughed. "I'm really sorry. Nash is sick, so I've been up since four."

I groaned. "Love you, brother, but I'm done with this call. I want to hold my woman for another hour."

"Love you. Bye—"

I ended the call and checked my volume levels before heading back into the bedroom.

I caught a glimpse of Taylor's ring. She didn't like taking it off, not yet, and any dread I had washed away. Honestly, fuck any worries because right here, this morning, in this room, I had everything I needed.

I slipped under the covers, moved Natty aside, and pulled Taylor into my arms. She shifted to her side, and I moved up behind her, my hand falling to her stomach.

"What did Mason want?" she asked around a yawn, her hand falling to cover mine on her tummy.

I turned mine around, lacing our fingers, and moved in even closer, settling. "Nothing important." I pressed a kiss to the back of her shoulder. "I love you. Sleep, babe."

Her whole body shuddered on a jerk, and I heard another yawn slip out from her, then she was dozing a second later.

Home. She was my home.

20
PRESENT

"It was that day."

The dogs. It was when Mason called me with the first warning about James.

I pulled back, looking at her face. We were still at Manny's. People were yelling around us, and I was pretty sure some were yelling *at* us, but right now, it was only Taylor and me, and I was remembering.

"When did you know?"

She was so pale, and she bit down on her bottom lip. "That morning, Mason called at five? That day?"

The dogs wouldn't leave her side, not to even piss.

"It was that day. You knew that day." My tone was coming out harsh, but I didn't mean for that. My mind was whirling. My blood was buzzing. I had so many emotions crashing through me, and my hands were starting to shake.

Holy fuck.

Taylor was pregnant.

And she was still shaking in my arms.

I cursed, looking and finding Nate and Heather watching me,

their faces set in concern. I gave a slight shake of my head to them. "I'm heading out."

Heather started for us. "Wha—"

Nate cut her off, "Sounds good."

The unspoken context was that Heather thought I announced we were married, and she didn't know what the hell was going on. Nate knew something else was going on, and it took precedence over this stupid shit drama.

I took Taylor's hand but pressed a kiss to her forehead, cupping the back of her neck. I whispered there, urgently, because holy hell, everything was changing after today, "I know you're shaking. I don't know why, but I love you." I squeezed her hand. "I *love you*."

I started forward, guiding her in front of me, our clasped hands resting low on her hip. Usually, I'd take the lead, but not today. All these people were behind us. I wanted as much of an actual block to whoever was going to come after us.

"Logan."

I swallowed a curse because we weren't even out of Manny's back section before Tate was trying, whatever she was going to try.

I stiffened, but then a presence moved in swiftly from the right. "Leave him alone, Tate."

That was Nate, and as I guided Taylor forward, stepping through to the front section, I spared a look over my shoulder. Nate was blocking her way, but then we were through, and I moved, taking the lead. I kept Taylor's hand in mine. We went fast through Manny's until we were in the parking lot. The door banged shut behind us.

"Logan—" Taylor started.

I shook my head. "Stop. Just wait. Wait."

I drove so Nate would get a ride with someone else, and I was hurrying Taylor into the front seat, then I was around and in the driver's side. After that, fuck. I had no clue where James would be.

We had him in his old room at the house, but knowing my disastrous dad, he was probably banging someone new by now.

Either way, I wanted total and complete privacy. I wanted no one to be able to find us.

I made a decision, hitting the turn signal.

"Where are we going?"

"Somewhere no one will look for us."

"Logan," she started again.

My heart broke because she sounded so sad, so resigned. Cautious.

I did that.

My hands started shaking, so I gripped the steering wheel harder.

Me. I put that there, in her.

The fear, sadness, resignation. She was cautious *with me*. Her. My teammate. My life partner. Forget the fucking roles of husband and wife. She was mine. I signed up to be beside her for life long ago, and she was scared right now because of me.

I had wholly and royally fucked up.

I spoke low and raw, "I am not angry with you, but give me some time. I need to digest some things and figure out the best way to say what I have to say."

She choked out a sob, so I reached over and entwined her hand in mine. Our fingers laced together.

I held her hand the entire drive.

21

LOGAN

"Why are we in Cain?"

I drove and just kept going until I figured out where I was taking her. Then it all made sense. I squeezed her hand, "Hold on. Please."

"Logan." A sigh from her, and that sadness was still with her.

Pain sliced through me. "Just hold on. Please." I was saying it gently. Tender. I needed to be delicate with her, handle her with care. She felt like she was going to break. I could feel it in her, just under the surface.

I did that. Fuck me. *I* did *that.*

I turned off, heading into a different section of town.

"Oh my God, Logan." She sat up, seeing where we were going.

I pulled in, went to the buzzer, and put in the code. The gates started to open and I asked, "You remember this place?"

"It was the old amusement park."

I drove in. It'd been abandoned back then. It wasn't anymore. "James kept us abreast of the changes. He wants Mason and me to take over his company, and maybe one day, we will, but when he was deciding what to do here, I asked him to refurbish the roller coaster, bring it up to date so it can still be used."

"You did?"

I shot her a grin as I pulled into a parking slot. "He didn't, but a couple of years ago, I invested, and *I* brought it back."

"Logan!" Her eyes wide, her voice in awe.

I had to take a moment, just a moment.

She was so beautiful. She always had been, always kind. It was the kindness that undid me.

"You forgave me."

"What?"

"Back then. You forgave me, and that's the day I realized I loved you. But I decided to fight for you on that roller coaster. I wanted you to rip me apart, and you didn't. You did the opposite. I'm a fighter. It's what I've known all my life, and you never gave me that fight because it's not what I needed. Since then, you've let me call the shots. You let me set the pace, and I don't know where I fucked up"—my voice cracked—"you've always let me be me, and I've always needed you. I leaned on you, and you let me, but fuck, Taylor. I have made a complete mess of everything if you—"

I had to stop.

The years started flashing in front of me.

Our first Christmas.

Graduation.

After graduation.

Moving to Boston.

We followed Mason there, all of us. Taylor came with. She did that for me.

"I'm so fucking sorry."

"Logan, no." She started to reach for me, but I stopped her.

I caught her other hand, now holding both of them, and I shook my head. "I didn't want to grow up. I didn't want to lose what I had. You should've left me long ago."

"Logan, stop." She was crying.

I was doing it again, causing her pain.

"I am so sorry."

"Logan, stop!"

"You were terrified to tell me you're pregnant." Not okay! I took her in, seeing the love there, the sadness for me, and I looked down at her stomach—my kid. *My* kid was in there. I dropped my voice low, barely a whisper, "I thought for a long time, and I wasn't quiet about it. You let me be me, but I wasn't letting you be you, and I have failed you. I've failed to be a partner in the way I should've been because I was so scared of failing to be a partner to you in the way James has been. That's on me. I have fucked up, but Taylor..." I couldn't look away from her stomach. Right there. In there. A part of me and a part of her, and holy hell, I was going to be a father.

A kid.

Wait.

My chest tightened. "It's not twins, is it?"

She laughed. "No, at least I don't think so."

I released my breath. "Thank God. I love Mason's kids, but the twins are little shits."

She laughed again. "Maddie called them that too."

I grinned, reaching over and brushing one of her tears away. "You thought I'd be mad?"

She paused, stilling, then nodded. "Yeah." The word left her in a rush. "I knew how scared you were to have kids, and yeah..." She drew in another breath, holding it. "You're not mad then?"

"No. God no." I reached over, letting go of her hand to place my palm over her stomach. "It's different now. Everything's different."

She stilled under my hand.

I leaned down, resting my head on her stomach, almost wanting to feel the kid, whomever he or she would become.

My God.

A mini-me?

Maddie was already enough, but she had mostly Mason in her.

I looked up. "If it's a boy, he's going to be a demon."

She laughed, more of her tears falling free. I was hoping they were from relief, and she combed her hand through my hair, cradling my head. "I'm prepared. We should set aside a bail fund."

Yeah. That sounded about right.

Man.

I'd never felt this. Not when Taylor first kissed me. When she told me she loved me. When we moved in together. Not even when we married. That'd been my best night, or I thought. Nope. Today was. Today was the best day of my life.

I looked up at her. "We're having a baby."

She smiled down, tracing her hand down the side of my face. Her eyes were tender. "We're having a baby."

It was done.

I was complete.

I took her hand, pressing her knuckles to my mouth, pressed a kiss there, but then I reached up. I pulled her down. Her lips found mine, and my entire world shifted.

"**L**ogan," Taylor asked much later, on a laugh when I lifted my mouth finally from hers. We'd moved to the back of the Escalade, and well, I hadn't totally changed. I was still me. She sat up, brushed her hair back, arranged her top, and looked around. "What is this place?"

I stole another kiss, going for the corner of her mouth. "It's this high-end hotel resort place. Of course, it makes a killing in the football season. I own a part of this. Felt right to bring you here today."

"It's completely empty."

I snorted. "Christmas. It's closed for the holidays." I pointed across the pond to a larger building over there. "Except the hotel part. That's open. Everything else is closed."

"Oh."

I moved up, pulling her to rest against my chest, and she leaned back, her entire body melting into mine. She murmured, "It's beautiful."

It was.

Cobblestone walkways. Lighted pathways and lighted trees. There was a waterfall—a wooden board walkway.

People could kayak, float in a simulated wave river.

There was a concert podium on another corner of the lot where they held concerts. An email floated around, talking about hosting a new music festival. They were in talks to have Sustain headline here.

But the roller coaster was the best part.

"Come on." I finished dressing and opened the door, sliding out and pocketing my keys.

"What?"

I motioned with my head. "I want to show you something."

Her eyebrows drew together, but she followed.

I took her down the walkway that went to the roller coaster, and as soon as we turned the last corner, she saw it. "Oh! Wow."

I shot her a grin because it was so similar to her first reaction when she saw it.

It wasn't decrepit anymore. It was brand spanking new, with added safety measures put in place because I had hoped to get Mason to ride on it one day.

Seeing us coming, a worker came out from a back warming shelter. Edgar. He rubbed his hands together, smiling at us. "Welcome. I'm glad you made it."

Edgar made it sound like this was a typical run-of-the-mill day for him and ignored that I had texted him once I realized where I was going. He agreed to warm it up for us, just for one ride.

"Hey, man."

He gave another nod before opening the latch for us to proceed toward the ride.

Taylor stopped, and I moved up behind her. "Uh, Logan?"

I laughed, pressing her to go forward. "It's safe. Come on."

"Uh..." Her hand went to her stomach. "I told you I was pregnant, right? So I didn't imagine the last few hours? 'Cause if I didn't," a shaky laugh left her, "surprise. I'm pregnant."

I chuckled but pressed her forehead. I was walking with her

by now. "I know. One ride." I lowered my head, nipping her shoulder. "Please."

Her laugh started, turning into a half-growl, but she moved forward in jerking steps. Her head turned as we passed Edgar. "I'm pregnant," she hissed. "Pregnant. As in that a child is inside of me. Got that?"

He was stifling his laughter, trying to keep a calm composure. "I got it, ma'am."

"Ma'am." She snorted. "Change that to Mother."

A laugh broke out from him. "Of course, Mother."

"That sounds about right."

I was swallowing my laughter, almost pushing Taylor the whole way into the bucket seat. She got in, another jerking step, and she turned, giving me a pleading look. "Logan, please."

I ignored that, backing her up, going to her shoulders, and pushing her to sit down—a gentle push.

She buckled, her knees folding, and she sat.

I moved next to her.

Edgar stepped up, clicking in the seatbelt and stepping back, bringing the bar down over us. He double-checked it, making sure it was set in place. He stepped back, going to the controllers, and I called out, "Make it go slow."

He gave me a nod.

"Yes!" Taylor called out. "*Really* super slow."

He cracked another grin before hitting a button, and off we went.

An inch.

Another inch.

And again.

Realizing how extremely slow we were going, Taylor expelled a sudden breath. "Oh. Okay. That's better."

It'd take us ten minutes to get to the top at this rate, but the slowest mode that I asked them to put in is what we'd do for her.

She watched around us. I watched her.

And when we got to the top, when Edgar stopped us, she gasped again. "Logan." Her hand found mine, squeezing it.

I knew what she was seeing.

"It's the same view from back then."

She tore her gaze away from it, turning to me. "Yes, it is." She gave me a loving smile.

I leaned in, my forehead going to hers, and I brushed a strand of her hair back. "It's the same view I was looking at when Mason told me to go and get my girl."

I heard her breath hitch.

I dropped my voice, whispering, "Just in case you need to hear the words, I am *ecstatic* that we're having a child. I'm scared. I'm nervous, but I'm happy. And I have loved you since our first year at Cain University, and I will *always* love you. Forever."

New tears glistened from her eyes as she whispered back, "Thank you. I love you right back."

I knew she did. That's something she always gave me.

IT WAS when we were leaving that she saw the sign.

"Logan!"

I laughed and started taking off.

"You named this roller coaster The Taco Taylor Coaster? Are you SERIOUS?"

FOREVER PRESENT

TAYLOR

We drove back that night, but Logan must've sent out a request or something. We went to the house, and we were left alone for that night, the next day, and a second night. No calls. No texts. Nothing. Total and complete silence.

But six a.m. on our second morning, the small respite was done.

Malinda was knocking on the door, and thirty minutes later, Mason called. The rest of the morning consisted of phone and video calls.

Mason gave us shit. And congratulations.

Samantha gave us shit. And congratulations. She was a little weepy.

Nate. Same as the others. Also weepy. Quincey was with him, but she wasn't crying. She was all smiles.

Matteo. Same. One tear.

Heather came to the house with Channing. He gave us congratulations, but Heather gave Logan the most shit. "It's about time." "What took you so long?" "Honestly, what *did* take you so long?" "You're the marriage dinosaur." And so forth.

Logan didn't have the quick retorts as he typically did. He

held me on his lap and smiled and laughed and kept holding onto me. I could feel him resting his cheek to the back of my shoulders at intervals, his hands under my shirt and firmly resting over my stomach.

Heather noticed the location, her eyes darting back to mine, but she didn't comment.

Malinda was alternating between huffing about not being invited to our wedding, being irate at Helen, and still wanting to twist 'the weasel's balls off.'

IT WAS that evening when the doorbell rang, and the door opened. "Logan?"

It was Nate.

He came in, holding hands with Quincey. He paused, seeing us in the dining room.

Malinda was there. Heather too. Channing left because someone skipped bail, and he needed to go 'hunting.' His words, not mine.

"If I knew you were doing company, we would've come earlier." Nate gave the rest of us nods in greeting.

I moved to the chair next to Logan, but he kept his hand on my leg, dragging my chair to touch his. Heather had started inspecting our closeness with more speculation in the last couple of hours, but she was also watching Malinda with the same look.

Heather did not seem surprised at Nate and Quincey's arrival, and when both dropped into two chairs around the table, all gazes went to Malinda, then to Logan, and everyone sat back. They were waiting.

I frowned.

Logan sighed, removing his hand and leaning forward. "I don't want to deal with Tate."

Ooooh. That's what this was about.

Nate's eyes widened, and he shot Heather a quick look, which she matched, but she didn't seem so shocked before he turned back to Logan. "Uh. Okay." He leaned forward, resting his arms on the table. "Gonna put my cards on the table here. James isn't my dad. He's not Heather's. He's not Quincey's. He's yours and Mason's, and he's getting scammed by Tate." He glanced to Malinda. "Did you tell him what Mark said?"

Malinda's mouth tightened. "Not yet."

I felt another entire body sigh from Logan, one that wasn't audible, but he asked her, his voice resigned, "What's this about Mark?"

Her eyes darted from Nate to Logan. "It's not really what Mark is saying. It's what Cassandra is saying."

"You still don't like her?"

If it was possible, her mouth got even tighter. She jerked her chin up. "She's grown on me, been through some stuff with her family, but she came forward yesterday. Mark got an earful from me on the phone about your dad. I was in a venting mood, and well, Cassandra asked around. You know they're related?"

Logan shook his head. "I didn't, no."

"Distant cousins, I think, but she was told by someone credible that Tate was having an affair with some banking CEO. Not James Kade. She knew someone at the hospital who switched paternity tests, got the results she wanted. It's a scam. That's what Cass is saying."

Normal Logan would've erupted or spewed some vow to take his ex-girlfriend down.

That didn't happen.

He was quiet, giving a slight nod before turning and locking eyes with me.

I saw it then. He was tired. I saw the plea too. He needed me.

I nodded, standing up and taking his hand. "If you all will excuse us?"

Crickets could've been heard. No one said a thing, not one thing.

All eyes tracked us, and I could feel the stunned silence as I led Logan up to his old room. It was a small trek, this house was so huge, but I didn't need to say anything once we were in.

Logan grabbed me in for a hug, almost crushing me, his head buried tight into my neck.

"Loga—" I started.

He dropped to his knees, his hands raising my shirt, and I took it, holding it for him. He stared at my stomach, his hands catching my hips and pulling me closer to him. Finally, he spoke, staring straight ahead, "I don't care."

God. My heart split open. He sounded so agonized.

"I only care about this one and you. I care about my family, I do, but I'm done. I'm tired of being the fighter. I—Mason has his family. Nate has his, and I've been waiting. Not anymore." He turned his head up, his eyes fierce.

Oh, man.

I sank to my knees, cradling his face. "Baby."

His eyes shuddered closed.

I leaned forward, my forehead touching his, my hands falling to catch his, and I held onto him. "You can handle your dad's stuff. I'm not going anywhere. Our baby isn't either. I don't know where this is coming from, but we're here. I'm not leaving you." I moved our hands, going to his chest. I could feel his heartbeat going so hard, so fast.

I didn't understand what was going on here.

"We're married."

He laughed, his heart slowing a tiny bit. "I don't know what's going on with... I, just, I just want to hold you. I don't want to deal with real life. I want someone else to do it."

Okay.

I knew what I needed to do.

"Do you trust me?"

He lifted his head, his eyes finding mine. They were clouded over, just a bit. "Yeah..."

I cupped his face. "Let me handle this. You stay here. I'll do what I need to do, and I'll come back to you. How about that?"

He frowned. "You serious?"

I nodded in one quick clipping motion. "Let me do the work right now. I can handle shit and come back to you. But you need to give me a bit of time. Okay?" I hesitated, then asked, "I will need to tell one person about the baby. Is that okay?"

"Who—" He shook his head. "It's fine. I trust you."

I pressed my lips to his before standing, and as he shifted, still frowning, watching me the whole time, I walked out into the hallway. Then I took a minute.

Okay.

He wanted his family, not to handle someone else's family issues. Totally understood that. So okay then.

I could make that happen.

Nate was waiting halfway up the stairs, standing to one side. He saw me coming and raised his chin. "What's going on?"

His tone was no-nonsense, straight to the point.

I stopped, knowing I was wearing a slight frown. "He—real talk?"

Another quick nod. "Nothing else right now."

"Logan needs someone else to handle this fight for him. He needs a time-out."

Nate's nostrils flared. "A time-out?"

"Yeah."

He cursed. "Why?"

I was getting this. I understood. I mean, my God. I'd been front row to see so many years of friendship and family love between him and Logan, but Logan wanted time with his family. This was coming from concern because Logan had never shown this side before.

Because of that, I kept my tone calm and held out my phone. "I need to make a call, and then we can go from there."

I got one step back before he said, his tone grinding out, "I want to know what the fuck's going on with my *brother*."

I held my phone up higher. "One call."

I hit the button, and the phone was ringing by the time I hit the hallway again.

Mason answered, "Taylor?"

24

LOGAN

I didn't know how or what Taylor did, but ten minutes later, she was back.

Coming to stand by the bed, she held my gaze a moment before she came to some decision.

She reached up, taking her shirt off. Her pants. Her bra.

I was in a race now, yanking my clothes off, and by the time she was naked and sliding under the covers, I was ready for her. I sank in and paused at the feel of her, being inside of her, knowing our child was growing inside of her too.

I used to use sex not to feel anything. Now I felt everything.

I leaned up, looked down at Taylor, saw her watching me right back, and began to move.

Her. Me. Our baby.

Perfect.

25

MASON

The call ended, and I had to sit there for a moment.

Holy shit.

Holy shit!

I got on the phone.

To Sam, "Book our flights. For everyone. We're going to Fallen Crest."

Her, "What?"

To my coach, who was sitting across from me, "I need a day."

Him, "You just had a day."

"It's family."

"You just had family issues."

"I need another day."

"No, Kade."

"I'm taking a day. Maybe two."

"Goddammit. I said no!"

"It's my brother."

"Logan?"

"Yeah."

Silence.

Him, "Well, fuck. I love that asshole. Fine. Take a day. Watch your tapes there! And do your workout. You can train there."

I was up and moving. "Thanks, Coach."

He hollered after me, "One day, Kade! One. Day. Do your workouts. You got me?"

I raised an arm. "I got you, Coach! Workouts. Tapes. One day."

I made another call once I got to the Escalade.

"Mason Kade?" she answered.

"You helped Nate sort some stuff out a few years ago. I'm wondering if you can help me too?"

"I'm aware. It's why I answered your call. Is Nate okay?"

"He is." Then I told her what I needed.

"You're in Boston?"

"I am. Flying to Fallen Crest as soon as I can."

"I'll have a file for you by the time you land."

Good. I was counting on it.

I texted Nate next.

Me: Coming to handle James. Leave Logan out of it.

Nate: What. The. Fuck. Is. Going. On?

Me: Find my dad. Find Tate. I'll let you know when we've landed.

Nate. WTF, Mase! He's my brother too.

Me: I know, but I'm the one who got the call. You know what that means, right?

Nate: I'm sure you're going to tell me.

Me: Taylor likes me more.

Nate: Dick.

Me: Wrangle up the a-holes. I'm heading back. You'll find out everything. Logan will want to tell you, that's why.

Nate: Fine. We'll get tabs on Tate. I'm sending Channing and his team to your dad.

I laughed out loud and called him, "You better make sure he tapes that. I want to see his face."

He laughed. "I will." His voice dropped low. "Is he okay? Just tell me that much."

He was referring to Logan.

"He's fine. He's good."

Nate sighed. "I gotta go handle this bitch now."

I smirked. "See you when we land."

26

TAYLOR

M orning sickness was a thing, and it was coming in fast.
When we got to see a doctor, Logan wanted to know everything.

Would my boobs get too sensitive?

How long could we have sex?

Any position that was unhealthy or healthy for the baby?

And then the obvious ones:

When was the baby due?

When could we find out if it was a mini-Logan or a mini-Taylor?

And then he pulled out his phone and went down what he had googled:

Symptoms as the baby grew? Was it one baby? Not two? He was adamant about that.

Specific symptoms we should look for? Tell the doctor?

What were the approved or to be avoided foods? He'd need that list asap.

Was exercise okay? And not of the sexual kind? He was also specific about those two differences.

Vitamins? Supplements?

How long will morning sickness last, and could the father also get it? Because he was feeling a little nauseous this morning.

And so forth.

All of that was before we even got to the routine exams and family health history part, all of which would be shared with our usual doctor, where I had another check-up scheduled the following week, just in case. Logan was also adamant he'd be going to that visit too, and every single exam or test or phone call that had to do with anything about the baby.

After the visit, I hit his hand away from my stomach as we walked through the parking lot. "Okay. First trimester we don't want people to know."

"What? Why?"

"Stress. We're supposed to be as normal as possible, and we can tell people in the second trimester."

He had a funny look on his face, his eyes still on my stomach. "You look hot. Like hotter than normal. It's the kid. Holy. You're one of those moms who look hotter when they're pregnant." He pointed at my face. "You even glow. Everyone's going to know! Because of you."

I swatted his hand down, rolling my eyes. "Watch it, or my hormones are going to come out and kick your ass."

"My ass, huh?" His eyes lit up, starting to smolder, and the corner of his mouth lifted in a grin. A cocky grin. "I bet you're going to be like a rabbit with sex. Some women are like that. They get pregnant and only want the dick." He reached down, cupping himself. "Taylor." He sounded so serious, but that half-grin was still there. "This is always at your beck and call. I need you to be reassured. You can ride me anytime you want. I'll talk to my boss, make some amendments to my contract."

I laughed but grabbed his hand. This was typical Logan.

A second later, he slid our fingers together, and there, right there, that touch alone settled everything. Not that I wasn't settled, but it was an extra seal. Perfection.

Then I remembered.

"Oh no! We were in Cain, and I didn't call my father!"

27

MASON

We arrived. Sam was confused but was going with the flow because a trip to see Heather was always a good thing in her eyes. Maddie was glowering at everyone. The twins were nuts. I was convinced Sam fucked the Energizer Bunny on speed because that's how nuts my kids were.

I thought Maddie was a lot, but she's a picnic compared to them. Nash brought home a goldfish two days ago. We don't have goldfish. We don't have any neighbors who have goldfish either.

Where the fuck did the goldfish come from? We asked, and he just shrugged and ran off again.

My kid.

They're both like that.

But we arrived at Malinda's house, and David greeted me at the door with a beer.

I now loved Sam's father because the dude understood. Or maybe it was me who understood.

Three kids. Fucking nuts.

"David!" Sam went in for the hug.

She did the hug. I took the beer.

I shook my head because that right there showcased us as a

couple.

"You look pissed?"

Sam was heading inside, going to find Malinda. The twins ran after her. I had no idea where Maddie was. We'd been here ten seconds, and she was already gone.

David added, "I mean, pissier than normal."

I raked him over, taking a long drag. "You look like you should be pissier than normal." I narrowed my eyes. "Bet you'd be pissy if I told you we brought Analise with us."

He paled.

I was wrong.

He didn't get pissier. On the contrary, he looked ready to crap his pants.

And I was a dick.

"I'm sorry. We didn't. That was uncalled for. I like you, and I don't know why I was just a dick to you." But I did know because we traveled non-stop, going commercial, and Sam was happy the entire time. She always got like this coming here.

Logan was here.

Nate was in Seattle.

My fucking father. I'd had time off. When I started playing in the NFL, everything changed.

All my old bullshit stopped. It had to, and Logan handled a lot of the drama that popped up for us regarding our family. He'd been almost on-call when Nate's stuff was going on. There was shit with Matteo that went down, and Logan went to help him with that.

Taylor called me, telling me what she told me. She was right to do that. Logan needed time with his family. That was precious and a very new time for them.

It was my turn to handle this.

Goddamn James Kade and whatever stupid shit he got himself into.

I hated my dad. I thought it'd gotten better, but it hadn't. I'd just been out of the game. Logan had been shielding me, but now here we were. Another drama because of James.

I growled, "You think shit changes, but it doesn't. Nothing fucking changes."

Maddie appeared, like magic, and had been walking past me into the house. She froze, her eyes big and turning to me. "Dad!"

Shit.

I clenched my jaw. "Sorry, kiddo."

She continued staring at me. Hard.

I growled but dug into my pocket and gave her a five-dollar bill. "Don't tell your mom."

She plucked it out of my hands and gave me a bright smile. Then, tipping up on her toes, she kissed me on my cheek. "Thanks, Pops." She turned, hugging David. "Heya, Grandpa!"

David's look was rueful when she ran inside. "You should just give her your entire wallet. I remember how you boys used to curse, and you haven't even seen your father today yet."

I didn't need the reminder because I wanted to let loose with all the swearing once again.

David helped me unload the rest of the vehicle, and when we got inside, he gave me a nod to follow him.

I followed, going into his office.

He went to the liquor cabinet, pouring a bourbon for both of us. "So. What's the plan?"

"I got briefed a little. Mark's woman is saying Tate's whole thing is a scam?"

His head got hard, and his chin moved up and down, real slow. "Those boys are both born and here. Four and six."

I cursed. Again.

Then glanced around to make sure Maddie couldn't hear.

The office door was closed, but that wouldn't deter her. If she thought this was a moneymaking trip, she'd have microphones placed in vents by now.

"You've seen them?"

His face was still hard as it moved left to right. "She's got 'em locked down, wherever they are. Malinda's been putting out the feelers around town. No one's seen 'em."

Which boded for the scam theory.

I tipped my head back, drinking the entire glass in one go.

Fuck.

Shit.

That stuff burned, but I needed it.

"Do I need to worry about Logan?" His eyes shifted to the door, which was still closed. "Can't help but notice his absence when I know he's in town. You two good?"

I threw him a frown, not expecting that one. "Yeah. He's got stuff going on right now, but I don't think he'll miss this. He just needs some time for a bit."

There was a brief knock before Sam stuck her head inside.

She smiled brightly at her dad. "Hey, Dad!" Her eyes were brimming. She was sparkling. She was so alive being here. Her gaze swung to me. "We're staying here for Christmas. I made the decision."

"I have a football game."

"You'll have to fly back for that. We're staying. Heather and I decided. You can take the red-eye back or book a charter, and we'll do an entire party this year. We're going to make Logan propose to Taylor in front of us because no way is he getting out of that tradition."

I grunted. I knew that was coming.

"Can you email the travel agent? I'll charter a private plane, there and back."

"Okey-dokey." She came in, coming to kiss me before hugging her dad. She called over her shoulder, "You better not be planning Tate's take-down without us. I'm just saying."

David laughed, finishing his drink and taking my glass. "On that note, Nate is over at the old house."

Time to get this shit handled.

28

GROUP TEXT

Mason to everyone: Heading to the Mausoleum. I got a file from Nate's PI on Tate.

Nate: About time. Get your ass over here.

Channing: James is rounded up. We went nice, at first. Where do you want the Pops?

Heather: Dump him in the ocean!

Samantha: I concur. Put him in his car and take out the brakes.

Heather: I concur right back!

Quincey: I feel like I'm supposed to be making a threat, but that's culture clash for me. Nova is all about loving everything. She'd be upset if that car hit an animal.

Samantha: A giant pool it is. Knock him out before he goes in.

Channing: Jesus, women.

Samantha: Five dollars! You owe me to give to Maddie because she just saw that last text come through.

Heather: Malinda is watching all the kids. I'm bringing drinks. FYI for everyone.

Mason: Channing, bring him here. Who's got Tate?

Nate: I outsourced. Blaise has a friend who knows where Tate is.

Mason: You didn't...

Nate: Not sorry. I did. He comes in useful sometimes.

Mason: Do not let that stalker know I'm here, but we need to talk with James first, then her.

Nate: He's harmless.

Mason: He didn't grow up with *your* picture in his locker.

Matteo: Wtf have I missed?

29
─────

TAYLOR

We were back in Logan's room, and I read through the group text. Logan and I were both included, but looking over, I didn't think Logan had even turned his phone on after our prenatal visit.

He came back from the bathroom, drying his hair from the shower, padding naked to his closet.

He skimmed a look over me before disappearing inside. "You okay?"

I had to make a decision.

I blacked my screen, putting my phone away.

"Mason is downstairs."

He came back, boxers in hand and his eyebrows up. "Say what?"

"I called Mason that day when you wanted time off. That's what I did to get it handled. I called him." My hands went to my stomach. "I told him about the baby."

"What?"

"I asked him not to say anything to anyone. I needed him to come in and head everyone off. So that's what he did. You walked out of a room. They're downstairs now, talking about a fight coming. I asked you to trust me. I told you I might need to tell someone about the baby."

"I didn't think you meant Mason."

I got quiet. "I'm sorry. I took that from you."

He closed his eyes, shaking his head as he went to the bed and reached for his phone. He turned his on but said as he waited, "You were right to do that. Mason is the only one who could hold everyone off. I, just, that's my brother. It's been him and me before anyone else came along."

He was right. He was *so* right.

I had fucked up.

"I'm sorry. I'm so sorry."

His eyes cleared, and he blinked suddenly, as if seeing me for the first time, and reached for me. "Hey. Hey. It's okay. I get it. I do." He motioned to me. "Come here."

I didn't, so he stood, grabbed my hand, and yanked me over to him as he sat back down. I landed on his lap, and he wrapped an arm around my waist, anchoring me in place. His phone started going off from the texts, but he tossed it behind him on the bed and only focused on me.

I closed my eyes, because man, I had seriously messed up. That was his brother. "Logan," I whispered. My hand formed a fist and pressed into his shoulder. "I'm so sorry."

"Taylor." He sighed, brushing some of my hair behind my ear, and he leaned back to see me better. "Look at me."

I did. Tears flooded my eyes.

He shifted his arms, moving me even closer to him on his lap. I was sitting sideways, but my ass was right over his dick, and I could feel it rising, pressing up against my pants. "Babe. I needed time to be with just you and our baby. It was a lot to process. All Mason got was a sneak peek. That's it. And trust me, it's killing him that he can't tell anyone. Knowing my brother as I do, he wouldn't tell Sam even, and that's *really* burning in him." He laughed, pressing his mouth to the back of my shoulder. "He's gotta keep the secret until the second trimester too. After that, I might be okay with how this worked out. He's like my shield. If I gotta check out, do pre-dad stuff, I can send everyone his way, and he's gotta handle it. I kinda love it."

His hand moved, spreading out over my stomach.

He whispered, pressing another softer kiss there, "Also, by the way, if you haven't gotten the memo yet, I've never been happier than now."

I shifted, turning my face so we were an inch away. "Yeah?"

He nodded, so solemn. "Yeah." He moved in, his mouth finding mine and opening over mine.

We kissed and made out like we were teenagers until Logan moved, almost tossing me on the bed, and started to crawl over me—that's when we heard the yelling.

30

MASON

"What is the meaning of this?" That was James' exclamation once he was brought inside.

We'd been ready, having had our meeting, and all of us were standing in the kitchen when I gave Channing the go-ahead to bring in the package. So he did, leading the way with my father being pushed behind him by Congo, one of Channing's guys.

A surprise happened when we saw that behind Congo was Channing's younger sister.

Over the years, we'd seen Channing's sister on and off.

I'd always felt some similarities with her and Samantha, but Bren was a different sort of animal. She was like a beautiful female wolf in human form. There'd been a feral feeling to her. Approach with caution. I felt it the first time I met her, and it was still there, though I knew through Channing that she was happy, married, and had a couple of children. I knew her husband, too, another member in her childhood 'crew' that was still tight to this day. Our group was close, but their group had a different sort of tight like they were half of each other. According to Channing, it never lessened. Where one moved, all moved.

I was guessing from seeing the slight reservation on Channing's face, in the way he tracked his sister's movements, that he still didn't know how his sister would react to being around us. She'd always had this mysterious but stay-the-fuck-away-from-me-or-I'll-slice-you vibe when she was around us.

I took one look, and yep, still there.

"Bren!" Heather squealed, heading over. She had her arms out, ready to pull her sister-in-law to her chest, but Bren held up a baton. Heather skidded to a stop.

"I have weapons on me. Hug gentle."

Heather was fighting a grin but nodded and stepped in, slowly wrapping her arms around the younger woman.

The guy behind Bren snorted and started laughing. "Only you, Bren. No one puts the smackdown on Heather. The woman's a legend."

Heather laughed, reaching out and flicking the guy's shoulder. "Hi, Zellman."

He sobered, fondness softening his face. "For the record, you never have to give me a gentle hug. Ever. And definitely *not* from you."

Channing took a step forward so he could see and glared. "Mine." He stepped up, looped a hand around the back of Heather's pants, and began pulling her backward. He repeated over her head, "Mine."

Zellman rolled his eyes. "So overbearing. It's not a good alpha look."

Bren closed her eyes, slightly shaking her head. But there was a faint grin on her face as she glanced to her friend, who threw his arm around her shoulder, moving to stand behind her. She settled back against him.

"Excuse me?" James started forward. "I said what is the meaning of all this?" He took another step, but a hand came down on his shoulder, and he was jerked back into place. He tried glaring at Congo, whose hand was like a cement block on his shoulder, but Congo was impervious. The dude was like a literal human-shaped brick, bald head. And the thing was that he wasn't even the biggest in Channing's crew. He had another humongous human named Moose, who was given the name for a reason.

"Stay." One word from Congo.

James looked ready to kill if he could.

That's when I stepped forward because it was time to get this going.

Everyone quieted, knowing the real show was about to start.

James sensed the shift in the room and turned, looking and finding me. "Son."

I opened my mouth, ready to start this thing, when a stampede of feet came from above us.

Down the stairs.

A whole different shift came over the room, a more alert, more viral, more frenzied air, and I knew who'd joined the fight.

I closed my mouth and held over the file from the PI.

Logan breezed past me, grabbed it, and went right to stop in front of our father.

He grinned. "Hey, Dad. Nice to see you again. It's been a few days."

I couldn't hold back a grin because that was my brother. He had processed his shit, and now he was back. He was ready to fuck shit up.

"First off, welcome to the Getting Fucked Over by Tate Club because you, my father, are totally and moronically getting fucked over by her."

31

TAYLOR

I followed him after he read through everything, saw what was going on.

The fight came back to him. He needed it. His energy was like an electrical outlet, surging and snapping and ready to strike out, *needing* to strikeout.

That was my man. Now he needed this type of outlet.

I sat on the stairs, able to see over everything and hear, and I leaned forward, my elbows resting on my knees as Logan did just what I knew he needed to do.

He took the file from Mason, striding forward.

Mason glanced around, then up, finding me. I could see the question in his gaze, looking me over, and I gave him a slight nod and smile in return. He gave me a mirrored nod before turning to what was unveiling before us.

This was Logan's forte. It was no longer Mason's. I saw that much in the relief in Mason's gaze.

"—moronically getting fucked over by her." Logan had started.

James frowned, starting forward.

Congo's hand held him back. James was on a tethered rope, and he was allowed only so much space before it would retract back into place. Congo could not have cared less about what was happening, but his job was to hold onto James Kade until told otherwise. That's what he was doing.

James huffed, and asked in a scathing tone, "Do you mind?"

Congo stared at him and blinked. That was all he did. He could've yawned, and his face wouldn't have changed.

"You got scammed, Pops." Logan started reading from the file. "Tate Sullivan wasn't just fucking you. She was screwing the CEO of Import Banking. Know Carlisle Scamponi?" He held over a picture. "Recognize him? Looks a bit like Evan and Owen, right? Carlis—wait, no—your sons?" Two more images were produced, and James winced as he saw them side by side.

He paled with the first image.

He paled more with the second two.

"Also, according to this file, Tate's been having a sexual relationship with a Benjamin William, and that will be important because guess where Billy works?" His usual cocksure smirk was firmly on Logan's face. "The Fallen Crest Medical Labs. It's where the paternity tests would've been done."

James was as white as a sheet. A slight draft could've knocked him over.

Logan flipped the file around. Another picture was pinned inside. "She's been banging him for eight years." He stopped, pinned his dad with a stern look. "What's she been asking for, Dad? I'm assuming money, but what else?"

James had to pull his gaze away from the pictures back to Logan.

He wasn't so talkative now.

He blinked, his body unsteady. "I need to sit down."

Congo and Bren moved in, both taking each of his arms and they walked/carried him into the kitchen. I had an even better view now. They put him in the chair that, if you looked up, you could see exactly where I was. The rest filed in after, and Logan glanced up, saw me, and winked.

I loved my man.

"What's she been asking for, Dad?"

He slumped over, shaking his head. "I had a paternity test done. It came back positive. They—" His head whipped up, he went from Mason to Logan. "They look like you both!"

"Probably why she picked the guy she did." That came from Mason, who was sounding more resigned than disgusted or pissed. "What'd she get out of you?"

"Shares. In the company. For both boys. She—she was adamant. Threatened to tell Analise about the affair, make it sound like I'd had two families behind her back. I haven't." He was looking at both his sons for validation. "I didn't. I didn't do that. I didn't know about the boys until eight months ago."

Eight months.

Man.

"I had the paternity tests done. They came back from the company, sealed." His head hung back down. "She was on the phone with me, wanting me to put the boys in the will. Analise overheard. That's how she found out. I—I was with her during those years when she would've given birth, but I didn't know she'd even been pregnant. It was only a few times, that was all. After the last time, I went to therapy. I have. I...I do love Analise. We're both flawed. I understand her, and she understands me, but this... I can't lose her."

"Analise is the least of your problems, Dad," Mason clipped that out. "Did you put them in the will?"

"No. Everything blew up. I haven't had a chance."

"How is Helen involved?" Samantha spoke up, moving forward. Her face was set too, firm and unrelenting when James turned her way. He grimaced, visibly shaken, when he saw her.

"I don't know."

"Da—"

"I don't know!" he cut off Mason before his gaze fell again. "I swear. I'm assuming Tate reached out. She's been threatening to tell everyone. I'm guessing she started with Helen."

"Fuck that."

Everyone turned to Logan.

He continued, "Fuck that. Mom knew, and she didn't call us?" He glanced at his brother. "Mom knew."

Mason's eyes widened. A normal person would've looked staggered from that statement. Not Mason. That was his only reaction—that his eyes widened. Then he cursed, long and low, and savagely.

Malinda was the 'mother' of the group.

Analise was Sam's, and I barely spent time with her. Logan preferred to stay away when Analise was around, but there were times we had a holiday meal with her. She was quiet, always watching Sam, a timid air to her. The two interacted, but there was a fragile sense to them, to their relationship. I knew what happened in the beginning. Logan had shared everything, but a part of me watched Analise, and I'd felt a weird crestfallen sadness.

In a way, Sam had a mom, but she didn't at the same time.

I ached for my mom—every day.

Sam also ached. I could sense it from her, and she was hurting again. As she caught my gaze, we were both aching for our men.

She'd been leaning against a wall, her arms crossed over her chest, but still holding my gaze, she pushed off slowly.

I was standing at the same time.

We were both on the same wavelength, and as she started to leave, Mason asked, "Where are you going?"

Logan saw me moving. "Taylor?"

Sam waited for me to come to the end of the stairs and answered for us. "We'll be right back."

"Fuck no. I'm in on this."

Heather brought up the rear.

We got one more surprise when we left the house.

Bren came too.

32

SAMANTHA

I never wanted to do this. In fact, I had gone out of my way to steer clear of Helen.

She was Mason and Logan's mother. She barely raised them, though I knew both loved her. There had been touching moments, a few, but this was too much. To team up with Tate? To scam her ex-husband? For what? What cost?

She hadn't told Mason or Logan for one simple reason—she knew they'd find out the truth.

I wanted to burn everything down around her. Her house. Her car. Her belongings. Whatever she prized most, I wanted it gone.

There was a memory coming to me as we got in the car, all of us piled together in one, but the memory was mine.

When I went with Mason and Logan. When they went to mess with Roussou's football coach at the time.

Roussou hadn't been the town it became later. I knew it wasn't bad or good, rich or poor, but I thought the town was doing okay. It turns out I was wrong. But my memory wasn't about Roussou. It was about me, seeing my dad's car, and being so angry.

I knew what I did that night.

I had that same urge right now, but I had nothing to lose back then. I had everything to lose now.

I still wanted to do some damage. Maybe it was just in me, something that nothing could get out of me.

"We have a plan?" Bren was the one driving.

We had started for mine, but she whistled and motioned for us to follow her to a gigantic Jeep. Once inside, she shot off a text, and when it alerted back, she started driving. She was a bounty hunter, so we were in her world, to an extent.

Taylor and Heather both looked my way.

"Got any firecrackers?" It was a joke. Somewhat.

Bren's calm and steady gaze found mine. She was unblinking, like Congo in the house. "Flashbombs work?"

"You guys can carry those?"

Her eyes shifted to Heather, who'd asked the question, and she didn't answer.

Heather's eyes got big. "Bren!"

Bren's phone went off, and she hit the button to read the text.

A second later, another truck sped up behind us and then fell back, keeping pace.

"That's Z. He's coming for backup."

Heather cursed. "This isn't a situation where we'd need backup. Helen's not a fugitive."

"Yet."

Bren went back to driving, though. She nodded to herself, taking a left turn. "So we don't have a plan. Okay."

"No knives."

Bren's calm eyes slid to Heather again. "Not in high school."

"I'm fully aware of that. You're a little bit too chill right now. I know what you're capable of."

The faintest glimmer of a smile showed before Bren went back to a blank expression, slowing and taking a right. We were nearing the house Helen used in Fallen Crest. Parking at the curb, she kept the doors locked.

"You need a plan. You can't go in there and start yelling."

Heather spoke for me, "*You* yell at fugitives."

Bren had been talking to me, but again, turned to her sister-in-law, inclining her head a little as she did. "All due respect, Heather, shut up."

Heather's eyes almost bugged out now. "You did not just say that—"

"You're in my world." Bren focused on me again. "I'll reframe my earlier question. Yes, normally, I can yell at hoity-toities, but you cannot. You're emotional. If violence breaks out, I'm inclined to let you hurt your mother-in-law, and I think since that's your children's grandmother, you might regret your actions later. Maybe. I won't, but I'm trying to be a good sister right now for both Chan and Heather. So. What's your plan?"

I had nothing. "Yelling at her?"

"Right. I'll do the talking." She hit the unlock buttons, and we all piled out.

Her friend Zellman was already outside, leaning against his truck, his bounty-hunting vest on. He flashed us a grin, coming to fall in line with Bren. "Nice to see you ladies decided to join me. It's a nice day for some ass-kicking."

Bren told him, "I'm leading this."

His eyebrows shot up. "What?" He stopped walking, then hurried to catch up. "Why you?" He gave us an uneasy look. "Uh, you guys sure about this?"

"I'd like to either burn down her house or explode all of her vehicles," I told him through gritted teeth. "So, yes. I'm sure."

Zellman froze before scanning over Heather and Taylor and then closed his eyes for a moment. "Okay then."

They both stepped up on the front porch. Bren was about to knock when her phone and her friend's phones both went off. They paused, reading their screens, and then shared a look.

"No shit."

A genuine smile lit up Bren's face, and she glanced at me.

I was taken aback.

Channing's sister was stunning with a sleek beauty to her, but she was also a little scary. The girl stabbed her principal because he touched her. And that was not an out-of-the-ordinary occurrence for her, but whenever she was around us, she was locked down. I figured it was how she was with anyone outside her group. I always felt she was a little like Mason in that regard, but seeing a genuine smile light up her face—I was speechless for a moment.

Heather groaned. She was not speechless.

"What just happened?" she asked, moving around.

"Your girl has a warrant out for her arrest."

Heather blinked, staring at Zellman, who then flashed his phone screen at her.

She gasped, grabbing it. "Holy shit! Holy shit!"

She read it right before Zellman snatched it back, and then he and Bren got ready. They stepped off the porch.

Bren was on a radio that I didn't know she had.

Heather turned fully around to me, shock slackening her face. "Tate was previously arrested in Vegas, and she missed court."

"What does that mean?"

Taylor answered for her, "That means she's a fugitive."

Bren was listening, glancing around. Her radio was crackling back, but I couldn't make out what they were saying.

"There." Zellman and her must've been looking for someone. He patted her vest and pointed to a truck parked further down the street. The door opened. Someone was coming out. The door shut and... Oh, no. Mason would not be happy about this.

His stalker was crossing the street, wearing a cocky smirk.

Bren groaned. "He's like the lint between your toes. You enjoy clearing them out but never know how the hell he keeps getting there."

He came over and stopped, scanning Bren up and down.

"What's up, Monroe? You gotta start admitting that you like me. It's been too many years. Cross and Blaise are all good."

She growled, jerking her thumb to the house. "Zeke. You followed her here?"

"I did. Put the word out. A buddy of mine saw her and gave me the heads-up. She's still in there."

"Who else is inside?"

Their radios both started going off, and Zellman stepped away, his head bending to listen.

As he did, Zeke answered Bren, "I don't know. Some old chick, and her."

"You don't know who?"

"Nope. You didn't ask for that."

Bren deadpanned, "I want to hit you. Right now. Right in the forehead."

Zeke's smirk just deepened. "But you won't because you've grown fond of me. Admit it, Monroe. Admit it."

Heather stepped toward Zeke, barely containing a growl. He hadn't noticed, nor had Taylor or I, and his eyes got bigger with each discovery, but Heather was in his face. He backed up. She went with him, and she lowered her voice, "I know who you're fucking right now, and if you screw her over, I will end you in all things Fallen Crest and Roussou. You'll have to go to Frisco to get gas, get food, get anything, and no one goes to Frisco anymore."

He didn't reply, just swallowed. His Adam's apple bobbed up and down.

Zellman came back. "Channing conferred with Hawk. We can take her, us two."

That was all Bren needed.

She pointed her baton at Zeke. "Stay here, or I'll use your proximity as an excuse to knock you out."

He stepped back, a wide step. His hands were up. "You got no qualms from me. I'm kinda terrified of this group now." He was side-eyeing Heather, but he didn't seem surprised by her threat.

Bren went to the door first.

Zellman was at her back, and he tapped her back.

She pounded on the door, "Open up! This is New Kings Bounties. We're looking for Tate Sullivan."

There was no response.

She hit the door again, "OPEN UP! NOW!"

The door swung open. Helen was there, and her mouth fell open. "What is going on—"

Bren shoved past her, hitting the door open and almost taking out my mother-in-law on the way.

I think I was in love with this girl.

Zellman went right with her.

Taylor.

I started forward and heard from Zeke as I did, "What's up, Mrs. Mason Kade?"

Heather put the palm of her hand on his forehead and pushed him backward. "Go away."

He chuckled, but I ignored him and went inside, already hearing all the glorious yelling from the two people I wanted upset.

Tate and Helen.

Christmas came early.

33

TAYLOR

I was running to catch up now because as soon as Bren shoved inside, someone went tearing through the house.

"Z!" Bren barked, but she didn't need to. Zellman sprinted past her. They split inside the house. Bren went left, and Zellman went right. Pounding footsteps could be heard outside, and a second later, there was a loud thud, and Bren was yelling again. "STOP RIGHT THERE! STOP!"

Zellman sped around the other side of the house. He was moving to intercept. A beat later, a whole cacophony of shouting was heard.

Heather and Samantha had stopped just past Helen, also trying to catch up.

I moved first, going by them and right back outside. I reached into my pocket as I did.

There, right there, the vision I was seeing was enough to make me come.

Tate was on the ground, Bren pinning her down with a knee between her shoulder blades. Zellman put a zip tie around her wrists behind her, and she was sat up once that was done.

Tate shoved up to her feet and started to run again.

Bren rolled her eyes and grabbed her, sticking a hand in front of her legs, but she caught her shoulders and eased her back down. She maneuvered Tate, so she was sitting, cross-legged, and the whole movement had been seamless and professional. I was impressed.

Zellman glared at her, standing in front of her. "Stay."

Tate glared right back.

Zellman laughed. "Good dog."

Okay, not so professional with that comment.

"Did you just call me a dog?"

"Better than what I want to call you."

Bren was on her radio, and as Tate started struggling, trying to make another run for it, Zellman moved into her space, forcing her back down, or she would've needed to hit his body to get away again. She fell back to her butt with a huff, more glares.

Seeing she was compliant, Bren moved a little further away, still on her radio.

Helen stormed past everyone, going to the front lawn. She started for Zellman, pointing at Tate. "I'm going to get you arrested for this. You're manhandling the mother of two of my grandsons."

"Actually," Sam spoke up, following right behind her and going around so Tate could see her. "She's not, Helen."

"What?"

I narrowed my eyes because Helen moved closer to Tate as if to protect her.

I moved in. "What are you doing?"

She swung her gaze my way, and a storm showed. Anger. Fear. Regret. But also indignant. What did she have to be indignant about? As long as I'd been with Logan, she gave no fucks about me. The only reason I hadn't cared is that she treated Sam nearly the same. Almost, but she was scared of Sam too.

Helen asked, "What are you talking about?"

I motioned to Tate. "You were just told by your daughter-in-law that the woman you're protecting *isn't* the mother of two of your grandsons. You asked the right question, but you moved to protect her. For what? Why wouldn't you want to know the information before going to guard her?"

"She's the mother to my grand—"

Sam was riling up, but I did a Logan. I spoke up first, "She's not, actually. If they're James's kids, then they have no relation to you. Don't know why you're getting that mixed up, but also Samantha was very clear in her statement. She." I pointed at Tate, who looked like she was envisioning my death, but I just waved at her instead, speaking to Helen, "Is *not* the mother of your grandsons. The real mother of your grandchildren is the one who just spoke, but you're still standing to guard Logan's ex against Sam." The more I spoke, the more my anger was churning. Finally, my hormones just woke up with an attitude. "You're a moron."

She gasped.

Heather started laughing.

Samantha was grinning too.

"Excuse me?" Tate's mouth dropped.

I rolled my eyes. "Please. You have no place to act self-righteous. Mason called in a PI. It took her ten hours to find all the other men you've been screwing." The glare lessened, being replaced by some caution. Her face got tight. She swallowed. I kept on, "The banker." The blood was draining from her face. "The guy at the medical labs in Fallen Crest." Even paler. "I'm betting if another paternity test was done, the results would be different."

Helen's eyebrows snapped together. "What's she talking about, Tate?"

Tate continued to hold my gaze. I didn't know why, if she was seeing if I was testing her, bluffing, but whatever it was, she saw, gulped again, and looked away.

Zellman gave me a once-over, approval in his gaze. "Nice."

"Samantha?" That was from Helen, who was looking from me to Tate and Samantha. "Is that true?"

Sam was also watching me, a thoughtful consideration taking over her. Her face went somber, and she raised her chin just slightly.

I don't know what got into me.

I knew Helen didn't like me. I never cared. She could think what she wanted. That was her problem. Not mine. But for her to guard Tate against Samantha? That made me want to take a taser to her because how fucking dare she?

I shook my head, turning to face her. "Samantha's had three of your grandchildren." I nodded in Tate's direction. "But you guard *her*? Her, who has a history of trying to fuck with Logan, Mason, and Sam. I can't believe you'd be so fucking idiotic not to do your homework, not to know what Tate's done. James cheated on you. He was cheating with her on his current wife, but you took *her* side? You doubled down on the cheater's side? You didn't reach out to tell Logan or Mason because you're not dumb. You did that for a reason."

Helen was silent.

That made me even angrier.

"Are you serious? Nothing? You say nothing now?"

"I know they wouldn't be my grandchildren, but they're new babies coming into the family. I wanted to be involved. I didn't want to get pushed out and I knew my sons. They'd bring them in as if they were their sons. It's how my boys are. I just wanted to be involved. How wrong is that?" Helen's lip was trembling. Her voice cracked.

Sam frowned. "Like you don't see your real ones now? We come here all the time. Mason calls you every visit, and you make time for them maybe once every eighth visit. He offers to drive them over to you. You've taken him up on that offer twice in the last four years. Maddie's not little anymore. She's aware of what grandma is in her life and which one isn't. She got confused the other night because we told her Malinda wasn't her grandma through blood. She was devastated. I didn't enjoy educating her on whose blood she actually did come from. Do you know what would've made that a lot better? If she had a better relationship with you."

Helen's lip continued to shake. "I wanted to start new with Tate's children."

"Start new? What happens to Sam's children?"

"Nothing. I mean, I'd continue—"

"No." Sam's laugh was bitter and cold. "I got it. I do. Have at it. I don't even want to share the news with you now. It's on you to ask your son about it. Good luck, though." She motioned to Tate. "Keep protecting her. And while you're at it, you might want to start kissing Taylor's ass." Helen cringed, but Sam kept on, "Everyone sees how you treat her. It's not much better than how you've treated me, but you're a piece of work. Alienate your daughters-in-law—"

"What?"

Sam ignored Tate, still speaking to Helen, "—who are with your sons that have no problem walking from you. It'd make more sense if they were different sons, mama boys, but Mason and Logan aren't like that. They put effort into who puts effort back in them, and that goes for their families too. I'm officially done. Here on out, you want a relationship? It's on you to try. I have other things to say, but I'm holding back because you *are* Mason's mother, and I know he does love you, even if he can't stand you at times." Her gaze went to Tate. Her voice was biting. "Have fun in jail. Knowing Logan, he'll find a way to keep you there. I'm out of here."

She turned, walking back to Bren's vehicle, pulling her phone out with her back pointedly to us.

Helen didn't react.

Tate was still seething at me.

I knew it then. A knot was in my gut, and it was tightening.

I said it, "That's why you did this? For Logan?"

Defiance flared in before she banked it. "No. That ship's sailed, but I care about Logan. Always will."

"Then why?" That came from Zellman.

"Money, you idiot."

He chuckled. "Right. The chick zip-tied from an arrest in Vegas, being caught in the middle of another scam, is the one calling me an idiot. Probably might be why you're where you're at."

"That's enough," Helen spoke up but quiet. Her face was tight. She looked in pain. "It's true? What they've all said."

Tate harrumphed, making a show of rolling her eyes. "The douche is right. You're the idiot. Of course, it's true, and you knew it. What Logan's current cunt—OW!"

Sam was back, and she had a knee on Tate's neck, pressing her down. "You will never call Taylor that again."

Tate went still, eyeing Sam.

She didn't move a muscle, not even as Sam lifted her knee, her eyes feral and her tone so cold. She stood back up, backing away slowly. "You've hurt my family enough." She turned, finding me. "Advice?"

I nodded.

"Walk from her. Right now. Don't listen to anything she's going to say, and tell Logan everything she's said so far. He'll dole out his vengeance, and she knows it." She skimmed Helen faintly, adding to me, "I'd also ignore this one from here on out too. Let Logan handle her if he chooses. She'll be the one regretting it, not you."

An Escalade pulled up to the street, and Sam went to it, visibly shaking.

I knew who was in the Escalade, and I waited. Just a bit.

Once Sam was inside, and the door was closed, the back window rolled down. Logan was there, watching me, waiting.

That's when I showed Tate. Lifting my phone from my pocket,

I showed her the screen. "Logan likes these pants, but they're worn. Raggedy. Still. Logan likes 'em, so I wear them for him. I won't always be able to wear them, so I figured why not today. Early Christmas present for him. But you know the great thing about these pants?" I showed her the pocket, showed her the bunch of holes that were there.

She knew. She paled again.

I flashed her a grin, raising my phone and hitting the stop recording button. "The best thing today about these pants? Logan doesn't need to be told about what went down because he saw the whole thing." I said to Helen, "He heard the whole thing too."

A door was shut from the street. A figure was coming toward us.

I knew who it was. Everyone else did too, but I added to Helen, "My mom's dead, so I had hoped to have a relationship with my significant other's mother. You *did* try at times. I'll give that to you, but then it all changed, and you stopped. I kept trying. You began ignoring me. I blamed myself. Now, seeing and hearing all this, I know it was never me. It was always you. It will always be you. And I'll be following Sam's lead from now on. If she freezes you out, so will I. I'm going to have her back just like she had mine. Malinda is Mom enough. She's ten times the mother and grandmother you are." That figure moved up behind me, skimming a hand up my arm, brushing some of my hair back, and I felt his lips touch my neck before Logan spoke, "We're doing a family Christmas party on Monday. You're not invited, Helen."

Logan took my phone, putting it in his pocket, and his hand found mine, lacing our fingers. He began walking back to the Escalade, tugging me with him. I saw that Heather was already inside.

That's when Logan had the last word.

"See you in court, Tate."

C hristmas was tomorrow.

Yesterday was a Kade family war because Tate was in jail. The new paternity tests were sent in. Helen was all sorts of regret. Analise was flying in but not staying with James. She was checking herself into a mental health facility because she stopped taking her meds. That facility was an hour from here.

Malinda was still livid.

David was quiet.

James was remorseful as well and a little bit weepy.

Mason, who was already back in Boston, led the fight from an iPad propped up on the table, but he didn't tear into anyone. Logan was also quieter than usual. He sat by me, keeping a hand on my leg. I knew he wanted to touch my stomach, but Quincey and Samantha had both started giving me thoughtful looks, so he stopped doing that.

Instead, like right now, as I was standing and looking out our window, I felt him come up behind me. A hand touched my hip, moved under my shirt, and slid around to the front of my stomach now. He fit himself right behind me, pulling me back to half lean on him.

"Merry Christmas Eve." He kissed my bare shoulder.

I reached up, catching his head, and slid my hand to the back of his neck. He stayed where he was, his head half bent over me, his mouth moving down my throat, and I groaned, tipping my head back for him.

"You feel better?"

My stomach clenched up just at the memory. After dinner, I went right to the bathroom and stayed there most of the night. Logan covered for me and came up to keep me company an hour later. He sat on the floor, rubbed my back, brushed my hair back, gave me a new washcloth when I needed it. For someone who worried about having kids, he was already setting the partner bar pretty damn high.

I nodded. "I'm better now. It comes and goes. The weirdest smells set me off too."

"Can I do anything for you?"

I released his neck, and as his head straightened, I leaned my head against his shoulder and grinned up at him. "You're doing it."

We stayed there, Logan holding me as I stood in his embrace.

"Your brother will be back after Christmas."

"Yeah. Sam's happy here. She likes being around Heather." He paused a beat. "Mason's happier too."

"His job is in Boston."

"His job is up for renegotiation soon."

Logan was stiff behind me, and I looked up at him again. "What are you thinking?"

His eyes found mine. "Talked to my boss. They told me I could work wherever I want if I'm considering opening up a firm wherever it is."

"And you know I can get a nurse job anywhere."

"Your dad is here or close to here."

"Nate's not here."

"Nate's not far away. Matteo too."

"Are you saying what I think you're saying?"

He shrugged against my back. "It's a ways off, but you never know for the future."

There'd been a couple of other conversations between the girls, but they were few and far between. It'd been a while since the topic came up again, but now it was from Logan.

"I'll go wherever you want to go. I mean it. You. The dogs. Him or her." I pressed on Logan's hand over my stomach. "You're my family. I go where you go."

His gaze grew somber, darkening. "Thank you."

35

LOGAN

I had a kid coming. I couldn't stop thinking about him or her.
Would I be enough?

Shit was different when Taylor told me. All the fears, concerns got swept away because the kid was here, and it was like the clouds opened up above me, and fuck, like a rainbow came down. It was cheesy like that, but I was a changed man.

Everything was different.

"Coming in." Sam's warning was a split second before she moved in behind me, at the kitchen sink, and hip-checked me to the side. She deposited a tray of dishes into the sink before grinning at me. Then frowning. "What's wrong?"

"Nothing." It was the truth.

I had everything, literally everything.

"Logan?" She raked a hand through her hair, her eyebrows dipping down. "You're freaking me out. What's going on with you?"

"I never thought I'd feel this."

"Huh?"

I wasn't paying her attention, but I knew she looked at me like I had grown an alien head. Or an alien dick. Either worked for me. But I kept on, "When you moved in, I was so angry. That anger's been in me all this time. Not because of you, but I first felt it when you moved in. Over the years it's been chipping away, but it's still with me. It's better when I'm with Taylor. I'm calmer, quieter. She lets me be that way. With you and Mason, it gets stirred up again. I never know why, but it's gone."

I looked.

Sam's eyes were wide and almost bugging out. "Are you feeling okay?" She touched the back of her hand to my forehead. "Feverish? Is this post-marriage flu?" Her frown turned to a grin. "That's usually code for something else, you know."

"It's not totally gone, but I never thought I'd feel as complete as I do right now."

There was silence.

Then a soft, "Huh. And I thought I was just coming for more eggnog." She whacked my arm with the back of her hand. "If I knew marriage would do this to you, I would've made you take Taylor to Vegas years ago. It's good to be happy, Logan. You're due, not that you haven't been happy this whole time, but it's time you let yourself accept it."

I was nodding, my throat swelling up, and blinking because I didn't need my sister to have more reason to tease me. Me crying would be a reason.

Too late.

Sam was blinking back her tears, and I raised an arm. "Come here."

She pressed into my side, and I hugged her. "Is there such a thing as marital hormones?"

Sam barked out a laugh. "No. That might be the bourbon in the eggnog. I swear that Malinda adds another shot every year we do this."

I laughed.

Malinda and David came over for the day. Everyone had to be in Christmas pajamas all day long. Maddie and the twins would get to unwrap the gifts from the grandparents, and Helen had dropped hers off this morning. James too, but both weren't here for the festivities. The Christmas Eve tradition was snacks all day long. The kids had a movie marathon, all Christmas movies, and dinner was a buffet. Sometimes it was catered. Sometimes everyone pitched in and brought a dish.

The kids loved it.

Then it was gifts.

If Christmas were in Boston, there'd be a snow fight during the day. Sledding. Ice skating.

We were here, so the palm trees in the back got multi-colored lights on them.

Tomorrow was similar, except Nate and I would hit the golf course though we both sucked at it.

The girls liked to go on walks together.

We'd watch Mason's game and then Matteo's game because it was scheduled for the evening. After that, there'd be more food and drinks, laughs. Monday was the big day. Everyone was coming over.

I had a surprise in store for Taylor too. It'd be arriving when Mason flew in.

But because it was today and I was still hugging my sister, I clasped her to me once more. "Love you, Sam."

"Indulge me a bit." Her smile turned soft, and she held up a finger. "Threesome fearsome."

I barked out a laugh, entwining my fingers around hers. "#Alwaysandneverforgetit."

36

CHRISTMAS DAY

Mason's team lost.

Matteo's team won.

Samantha got drunk and tried to act out her version of *Cobra Kai*.

37

KADE CHRISTMAS

MASON

I t was hellish early in the morning when I arrived.

"We'll walk your dogs for you, sir." The flight attendant gave me a brief nod and smile as I started to depart. The other attendant was staying with me, but I nodded back. "I appreciate that. Just make sure to bring them back."

She gave me a funny look, but she'd find out. Or no. I hoped she didn't.

I didn't correct her about the 'my dogs' part. They were Logan's dogs. I was bringing them with me as a surprise for Taylor, but my brother owed me. These dogs. They were insane.

Matty wouldn't leave the car when we got to the airport, not because he was scared but because he wanted to keep going on a car ride. The dog was a freak about car rides. And Natty insisted on licking everyone. This dog was an escape artist. He kept getting out of his collar and running around to anyone in the area to greet them. A kiss. Lick. Tail wagging, and he'd go on to the next one. I tried with a harness, and he slipped that too.

Fucking needed to set up a camera on him. Of course, that'd get millions of views, but then I resorted to a harness, a collar, and I wrapped a leash just to connect the two. But I wasn't chancing anything. I kept a firm hold on his leash the whole time, only letting up once we were in the air, and I knew there was no way he could figure out his way to the cockpit to say hi to the pilot.

I was leaving the plane with my bag when an SUV pulled in. Matteo was at the wheel, and he parked, getting out to come over and grab some of my stuff.

"Hey, man." He threw me a grin, putting the kids' bags in the back.

"Hey! It's good to see you." We hugged each other. Matteo and I didn't get to see each other that often. His schedule kept him busy, and the same was for me. The off-season was our only free time, and that filled up real quick too. Family events like this were always worth losing any sleep.

I'd missed the guy. "Grace is coming?"

He got quiet before shaking his head. "She got a job promotion, so she's taking it. It's in London."

"Oh, man."

"We ended it, and she's dating someone else."

"She's over there already?"

"Went early to get set up. She's staying with a friend."

"Sam never said anything. I'm sorry."

He shrugged. "It's... whatever. I don't think she told anyone, just packed up and went."

He looked away, and I was taking that as a clue that he didn't want to talk about it anymore.

I put Sam's items in, then stuffed my bag in at the end.

"Mr. Kade, sir." The other attendant was coming down from the plane, all the things I needed for the dogs. I took the items, saying, "Thank you for everything."

"Thank you, sir. Thank you for flying with Elite Lines."

Matteo and I had worked it out before our games. We were both working on Christmas day. He had plans with his family after his game. I needed to fly in, so we decided on a good time.

The plan was to show up hella fucking early, and since he was driving, he offered to pick me up.

"Dude. You're carrying dog food and a roll of poop bags." He looked around. "There's no dog here."

I flicked him off. "Too early for your smart shit." I nodded toward the attendant who was bringing Matty and Natty back with her. "That one dog is a lunatic."

Even now, Natty was twisting around, raising his front legs and doing a body twitch. He looked like he was learning some new dance, but nope. He was trying to get out of the harness/leash combination.

Matteo burst out laughing. "You're a brave guy. You traveled with both of them."

I was eyeing Natty, seeing he got the collar off. It was hanging and dragging next to the harness, but Natty was doing a whole head twitch, and he was trying to flip his body around.

I swore as I went forward to grab him before he got loose. "I need a padlock on this dog."

The attendant had no idea how to handle him either. That was obvious. She didn't notice me approaching. Natty was on the ground, rolling around, and he had one of the harness legs off him. Her mouth was open, and she was trying to pull on the leash. "Come on. Don't do that. Oh, dear."

She started to reach down, but I got there first. "I got him."

Her head jerked around, flustered. "Oh. Thank you. I mean," she grimaced. "I'm sorry. I didn't see you there."

I took both leashes, and she hurried back to the plane.

Matty saw the SUV and Matteo, both of his favorites, so I let his leash go. He took off like a bullet.

Natty had paused, back on the ground, two legs extended out and his other front two paws up and twisted. He had crazy eyes, but he was watching me, his tongue hanging off to the side of his mouth.

I knelt, putting the harness back on him. Snapping my fingers, "Up."

He stood up, panting, and I knelt to pull the leg through his loop. He kissed me, running his tongue up my face from chin to forehead. He panted and did it again.

I grunted, "Lunatic." I stood, holding the leash. "Should've been named Loony."

He had no comment.

Matteo was shaking his head, laughing as I walked back with Natty.

The back door was open, and Matty was sitting perfectly, right behind the front passenger seat.

"His dogs are nuts."

"Uh. Isn't that why he picked them?"

I laughed. "Logan's soul dogs. I should buy him an alpaca as payback for Christmas next year."

"If you do, you need to do two. They die from loneliness."

"Even better."

We were in the SUV and pulling away from the plane.

Matteo glanced over. "You know he'll just give it to Nate somehow. Nova will see those things and fall in love. So you're really gifting Nate two alpacas."

I grimaced. "Maybe I'll hold off."

"I heard Mark's coming today too?"

"Yeah, I think so."

"What's going on with them, anyway? He and that girl still together?"

I shook my head. "I have no idea. Sam talks to Mark, but he doesn't talk about his woman at all. From when I was here earlier, I think Malinda is trying to like her."

He whistled. "Mark should just cut ties, make a start with someone new. They don't have kids?"

"As far as Mark knows." It was meant as a joke, but considering the earlier reason for my visit...

Matteo grunted, "True."

We talked about our teams, teammates, but nothing specific. General stuff.

Matteo was closer to Nate and Logan, but he and I were on good terms. It really was good to see him. He was family. Then we arrived, and as soon as we parked and I opened the door, an excited but shrill scream came from the house.

"DADDDDDDDDDDYYYYYY!"

Matteo started laughing. "Everyone's awake."

"Merry Kade Christmas."

The front door burst open, and two of my kids came running down. Maddy was chill, hanging out in the doorway, and she raised a glass of what had better be hot chocolate in a salute to me.

Then she saw Matty and Natty.

"OH, MY GAWD! MATTY AND NATTY ARE HERE TOO!"

38

TAYLOR

Kade Christmas ensued.

    I saw Matty and Natty and started bawling. Hormones.

Logan whispered, hugging me, "Surprise!"

Matteo was there. Logan was happy, jumping on him later. The SBC-er chant was heard throughout the day, but not by them. Maddy heard about it and taught the twins. Then, when Heather and Channing came over, the rest of their kids heard about it too. It was a whole choral piece with altos, sopranos, and someone tried for a bass. It didn't work.

Quincey and Nate arrived halfway through the day. Nova was in tow, along with the rest of their family too.

It was an entire event.

The older kids had settled in the corner, going over their presents and their phones. The rest played with Quincey and Nate's youngest, who was starting to crawl. Nova got wind of alpacas somewhere and wouldn't leave Uncle Mason's lap, asking about the alpacas.

Natty was loving life, on a continuous loop going from one

person to the next, giving kisses. Licks. Asking for pets. His tail never stopped moving. That dog would be exhausted for three days after today, but Matty knew better. He had snuggled onto my lap, his head on my leg, and I was petting him.

I was content watching everyone. I was seeing life, love, and hearing laughter.

I was watching happiness.

Then a hush came over the group.

Goose bumps rose, covering my arms, and one by one, all eyes turned my way.

"What?" I sat up straighter. Matty readjusted but didn't leave my lap.

Sam was blinking away tears.

Heather had a hand over her mouth.

Maddy gasped. "Holy shi—"

"Child."

"Sorry, Dad."

And then I saw as Logan came around the corner. He was holding an ornament in one hand and a sparkler in the other. It was lit, which sent some of the adults in a frenzy, grabbing their kids out of the way.

Logan ignored them, coming my way.

I still couldn't move. Matty was dug in. He wasn't budging, but he moved his head to watch his dad's approach.

"What are you doing?" I asked, but then I saw what was inside the ornament. It was a ring. *Another* ring. "Logan."

Air left me.

I started blinking away tears.

My throat had swollen.

My chest was pounding.

"Logan," I whispered.

He knelt, holding that sparkler out of reach since Natty had come over to try to help. "So there's a family thing. We're supposed to propose in front of everyone, and well, we didn't go that route."

"Cheater," Heather yelled.

Logan grinned but extended the ornament to me. He nodded at it. "You already have your ring. We already got married, but that's a memory for us. This one is for the family." He held it up. "Will you marry me, Taylor?"

I took the ornament, my cheeks hurting from my smile. "I'd *love* to marry you." I moved in, hugging him, and for a moment, it was just us. A ripple of tension eased from his body as I held him, and I leaned back. "Were you actually nervous?"

He gave me a look. "Um, yes. I'm proposing to you."

"Should've said no before the ceremony, Taylor." From Nate, his hand cupped around his mouth.

Quincey added, "She could this time."

"Wait!" Maddy shoved to her feet. "What? Are you already married?"

Max's eyes got big. He was sitting by her but eyed her balled hands and started looking around. Without missing a beat, Channing reached forward, grabbed his son by his shirt, and pulled him back and out of swinging distance.

"Uncle Logan!"

Maddy was fierce.

"Uh." Logan glanced my way before saying, "We are, but nothing official until the whole family witnesses the wedding."

Maddy was blinking, confused. "So you're not married?"

"We did a ceremony, but it wasn't—"

He was struggling, shooting me a look. Sam, Mason, anyone.

I spoke up, "Maddy."

She glared my way, but it was less fierce. She had a soft spot for me. I had one for her too. "Would you be my bridesmaid for the wedding?"

She gasped again, but her eyes were filling up with tears. The change was dramatic but genuine. "Really?"

I nodded. "If I'm doing a big wedding, I won't do it without you."

"Aunt Taylor!"

She started for me, tears sliding down her face, but Mason caught her and nodded at us. "Considering there's a live sparkler going, let's let Logan have the floor for a bit longer."

"Oh." She blushed. "Yeah. Sorry, Uncle Logan. I love you, Uncle Logan!"

Logan was still holding the sparkler as high in the air as he could get. Thank goodness for the tall ceilings in this Mausoleum. He cleared his throat. "As I was saying, now everyone shut the f—eff up!"

One of the twins gasped. "He said a bad word."

Nova's whisper was heard, "They always say bad words. Just go with it. Keep a tally and hit your parents up at the end of the night."

Smothered laughter came from the room, but Logan was now cursing under his breath. He leaned in, his forehead finding mine, and he whispered, "I brought this sparkler to torch the bottom of the ornament, make a whole gushy thing about it, but now I just want to drop it and torch the house."

I laughed, hugging him. "Don't give in to your delinquent side. Keep the faith, brother."

He tipped his head back. "Excuse me?"

"I'm pretending to be an SBC-er. Chill. Zen it out of you and proceed. You want to torch the ornament?"

He snorted, laughing, but then got serious. "Yes. From early on, you were my sparkler, bringing a whole new life to me, and I want to singe the bottom of this ornament. It'll go up on this tree to commemorate the first of another new chapter in our lives." He stared at me, and then dropped his gaze to my stomach and back.

Oh. OH!

I was back to fighting back the tears because my whole body was melting.

I nodded, tears streaming down my face. "I got it. I love you."

His own eyes got a little wet, but he stood, touched the sparkler to the bottom of the ornament until it had darkened. He handed the sparkler off to Nate, who dumped it in a bucket of water and set that aside.

"Dad! Are there fish in there?"

We heard Quincey replying in a hushed tone, but Logan went to the tree and hung it up. He turned, addressing everyone. "I love each one of you guys. Adore some of you more than others." He winked at Maddy, who was now all smiles and laughing. "But you all are my family. Each of you, and I know I went around the family tradition with you know, but it truly means the world to me to have everyone here together. I know life is going to keep going. Who the f—knows what will happen with James and Analise, but it'll happen. Promotions. Jobs will change. I'm sure more babies will come, but we're here. All of us. Together. I've had you guys all my life, and we just keep adding on. I love you all and Merry Christmas! #KadeChristmas"

There was laughter. Cheers.

The hugs started.

Logan was being hugged.

I was being hugged.

Natty jumped on Matty to get to me, so Matty had to get up. I was able to stand up for the hugs after that.

Logan found his way back to my side, one of the twins clinging to his back, and he pulled me to his side when we heard the front door open.

"We're here! Late, but here." Malinda led the way, coming down the front entryway and rounding to a stop at the living room opening. David stepped in behind her. Two more came next, Mark and Cass, who were holding hands.

That's when Malinda sniffed the air. "Why am I smelling fire?"

A beat of silence.

Then from Maddy, "THE TREE IS ON FIRE!"

If you enjoyed A Kade Christmas, please consider leaving a review!

They truly help so much.

Until then, for more stories head to www.tijansbooks.com

ACKNOWLEDGMENTS

I feel like I need to acknowledge Logan himself here because if he hadn't randomly popped into my head one Saturday morning, and be a pest, this novella might not have been written. I had no plans on this novella, but yep. It happened exactly as I said, and all the Fallen Crest gang were eager to join as well. Then the Crew crew started talking, and well, you see what came of it all.

Good old Tate and James, right?

I'm not usually big on writing time jumps, but this was how the novella was coming to me and so I decided to go with it. Blame Logan, if you'd like!

Also, a big huge thank you to the readers who have loved Fallen Crest and now Crew over the years and to the new ones who are discovering them. When you send me a message, email, or do a post in the reader group, you guys are keeping them alive. Not that they aren't, or... You know what I mean.

Thank you to the team that helps me on a daily too!

And lastly, thanks to my Bailey. He's always happy to give me a cuddle after a long day of writing. Love you, B.

KESS

One more step would mean certain death.

The words were scribbled on a piece of paper, taped to a bathroom stall, and I was about out of patience. I ripped it off, balled it up, and tossed it into the garbage. I knew why they put the note up, because this was the druggie stall.

Asshats.

There were three other stalls open, which wasn't normal, but we were in the end run of the school year. Graduation was in two days. It was our last official day of school, though most seniors stopped coming a long time ago. Not me. I was here because of *detention.*

Detention.

I growled under my breath.

I was about to head inside the stall, find the drugs I knew were stashed somewhere, and I was going to mess with them. I was going to hide them somewhere else in the bathroom, but just as I hit the door to open, the main door to the bathroom swung wide.

In walked Tasmin Shaw.

"Hey, Kess."

I paused, trying to stomp down some of my irritation. It wasn't her fault I was here for detention, but it was her brother's and his whole group's fault. There was a situation they brought about that ended with me getting detention. It was a whole round-about thing, and it didn't really matter in the long run. But, I couldn't be mean to Tasmin Shaw, or Taz as she was called by her friends. There were a few different reasons why I wanted to, but none really had to do with Taz as a person.

One, Taz was nice. Like actually nice.

Two, she was connected. Taz was not only popular, but she was well connected with the toughest crew still going strong in our school. We have a system, or *had* a system. There used to be a whole chain of groups that weren't gangs, but we weren't all friends either. We were in the medium between those extremes, and tended to look down on those who weren't in a crew. That meant you weren't loyal, and if you were crew, loyalty was like blood to us.

You needed it to be crew, or you were simply 'less than.'

Or I used to think so.

And three, there was a respect issue here because Taz's brother's woman was now the *only* female in a crew. There'd been one other girl, but no more, and I can say that because it was me. I used to be in a crew. We weren't big or even tough, but we were a crew and I loved my crew.

Now we were nothing.

"Hey, Taz."

She stopped before going into her own stall, noted where I was standing, and raised her eyebrows. "You okay?"

I'd forgotten what I was going to do.

"Yeah. I'm good."

Taz gave me another smile and went into her stall.

I moved inside mine, and a second later, her voice came through the room. "Do you have any plans for the weekend?"

The weekend. Shit. I usually did, but that was before my crew broke up.

Now, "Not really. You?"

Her toilet flushed—when had she even pissed? A beat later, her door opened, and she went out to the sink. Me, I was still standing just inside my door. I hadn't even closed it behind me, so here we go I guess. I nudged it back open, edging farther out as she washed her hands. Her eyes found mine in the mirror.

An emotion flickered in them, and oh no.

I was already readying myself, because whatever that was, I didn't like it. My gut was tightening up.

"You know, I heard that Zeke Allen from Fallen Crest Academy is probably going to throw a rager. They party almost every night over there."

I wanted to snort in disgust, or at least disdain. I didn't.

"Yeah?"

She nodded, finishing up drying her hands, and stepped back from the sink. "Where are your guys? Usually they'd be out in the hall if you're in here."

There was the whole gut tightening again. Right there.

I jerked a shoulder up. "They're out doing their thing. I'll catch up with them later."

"Are you dating one of them? Monica mentioned that one time."

"Monica doesn't know anything."

She was referring to one of her friends, who truly didn't know shit.

"Oh."

Those eyes of hers. Tawny and hazel, and there's a reason she and her brother were some of the most ridiculously good-looking people in our school. It wasn't fair. But the kindness and concern were what was really setting my teeth on edge.

I didn't need her pity.

"Anyways," I blasted her with a bright, but dismissive smile, "I gotta go to the bathroom. So..." Enough said. I moved inside my stall, shut the door, and sat. Then I waited.

That was rude.

I was feeling like an asshole, but a moment later she was edging for the door. She was going slow, and that tugged at me because Taz Shaw wasn't known for moving at a slow pace. She bounced. She hurried. She darted. She didn't move slow, and she wasn't my friend.

The door swished open and closed, and I cursed under my breath.

But, what? Go and attend a rich asshole's party tonight as a tagalong? I wasn't a tagalong. I'd never been a tagalong, and fuck if I was going to become one.

But because my day was still in the toilet (lame humor), that didn't mean I couldn't mess someone else's day up, too.

I found the drugs, but I didn't hide them. I flushed them.

Then I went to my last detention of my high school career, and that sucked too.

I wished I hadn't flushed the drugs.

You can grab the rest of Kess's short story, here!
Or go to www.tijansbooks.com

ALSO BY TIJAN

Related books:

Fallen Crest/Roussou Universe

Fallen Crest Series

Crew Series

The Boy I Grew Up With (standalone)

Rich Prick (standalone)

Frisco

Other series:

Broken and Screwed Series (YA/NA)

Jaded Series (YA/NA suspense)

Davy Harwood Series (paranormal)

Carter Reed Series (mafia)

The Insiders

Mafia Standalones:

Cole

Bennett Mafia

Jonah Bennett

Canary

Sports Romance Standalones:

Enemies

Teardrop Shot

Hate To Love You

The Not-Outcast

Hostile

Young Adult Standalones:

Ryan's Bed

A Whole New Crowd

Brady Remington Landed Me in Jail

College Standalones:

Antistepbrother

Kian

Contemporary Romances:

Bad Boy Brody

Home Tears

Fighter

Rockstar Romance Standalone:

Sustain

Paranormal Standalone:

Evil

Micaela's Big Bad

The Tracker

More books to come!

CPSIA information can be obtained
at www.ICGtesting.com
Printed in the USA
LVHW102230181221
706604LV00012B/417